MEMORIES OF EVIL

Memories of Evil

AN ABC FILES MYSTERY

Paul Masson

Paul Robert Masson

THE ABC FILES *by Paul Masson*

eBooks

In Paperback

Author's Note

I am grateful to the Niagara-on-the-Lake Writers' Circle–especially Eileen Campbell and Richard West–and my wife Betsy for helpful comments.

After World War II, the Allied powers divided up Germany into four zones, which a few years afterward became two: West and East Germany. The Eastern zone was part of the Soviet Empire, but with its own government that enforced absolute loyalty to the regime through the Ministry for State Security, or Stasi. Its repressive activities, which are widely documented, have cast a long shadow.

In the Western zone, British forces were given the name British Army of the Rhine and the Canadian occupying forces were initially attached to it. In the late 1960s, Canadian Forces Europe were reduced to an air base at Lahr and an infantry unit in Baden-Soellingen. They were disbanded in 1993 with the end of the Cold War.

Though much of the German background for the book is based on historical fact, the characters in this book are fictitious. Any resemblance to persons living or dead is accidental.

1

Prologue

Leipzig, East Germany, July 1986

Despite the oppressive Communist regime of the German Democratic Republic, or GDR, the Thomaskirche in Leipzig continued to perform Johan Sebastian Bach's compositions. The church organ and choir rang out with the music of the great composer, who had spent two decades there producing some of his best-loved works. Gottfried sat in a pew on Sunday, marvelling at the music and forgetting the dreary life that he would return to once he left the church.

He was a clerk in a bank, with a wife and a young daughter. He was lucky to have a steady and well-paying job–at least by the standards of the GDR. After high school he had taken courses in accounting, and now, at age 30, he was the deputy head of the bank's records department and could hope to succeed the current head, who was nearing retirement age.

His vacant gaze roamed while the fugue's notes filled his mind. It surprised him to see Jürgen, one of his colleagues from work, staring at him. He gave him a brief nod, then looked away. Why was Jürgen here? Was he following me?

A few days ago at work, Gottfried confessed to wanting to get a copy of a recent Deutsche Grammophon recording of Bach's Mass in B-minor. Since it was produced in West Germany, the record album was strictly out of bounds to East Germans. Indeed, it was treasonous even to admit to admiring such things. He imprudently confided to Jürgen his hopes that the GDR might loosen up access to cultural goods. After all, Bach was a universal inspiration for all lovers of music, and his glorious works made Leipzig justly famous.

Gottfried had obviously gone too far. He was aware that the Stasi–the Ministry for State Security–had informants everywhere. Anything but strict obedience to and praise for the regime was cause for suspicion. The Stasi could destroy your life merely because of a rumour or an uncorroborated denunciation. He just hoped that Jürgen was there for the music and not because he intended to denounce him.

The next day, when Gottfried arrived at work, he was asked to report to the Director of the bank, who was sitting behind his desk in his office. To his right was a tall man wearing a trench coat. The Director addressed Gottfried sternly. "You have been accused of attempting to acquire prohibited goods. I'm afraid that I will be forced to let you go, because such activities will not be tolerated here. Pack up your things and leave."

Gottfried did what he was told to do and went home to his wife Hannah and his daughter Emma. Hannah wrung her hands.

"What will we do without your salary? We have no savings! You have to find another job!"

He tried several agencies where he knew that accountants were employed, and offices which might need a clerk. None of them would even discuss with him the possibility of a job. The Stasi had done its work. Anyone who attempted to aid a traitor would immediately fall under suspicion and be at risk of facing the same fate.

Gottfried, Hannah, and Emma tried for a time to live on the vegetables that they grew in their garden. But two months later, with winter coming on, Hannah took Emma and moved back to live with her parents in a neighbouring village. Gottfried gave up his apartment and left Leipzig for the countryside. For the next few years, he would survive only by doing odd jobs on farms and stealing food. He never saw his wife and daughter again.

Bielefeld, West Germany, September 1988

"Tell us again, Sergei, why you came to us," the MI6 man said in German. The three intelligence agents–British, American, and West German–were sitting at a long table opposite the man in an interrogation room located at the British Army of the Rhine headquarters. At the side of the room were various assistants. The CIA agent had an interpreter behind him, in case his rudimentary German missed some of the subtleties of the conversation. Sergei noted that a pretty young woman wearing a pink skirt and a white blouse was sitting behind the MI6 agent, and had passed him a note. She saw Sergei looking at her and she gave him a quick smile before her gaze returned to her notebook.

The man sitting opposite to the intelligence agents was in his thirties. He had a broad face with the open expression of someone with nothing to hide. "As I said, I was groomed by the Stasi to go over the Wall and burrow into West German society. A mole, if you will. Like Günter Guillaume. All along, I saw this as my chance to get out of East Germany. When it finally came, I contacted your services to make myself available. I'm willing to tell you everything you want to know about my country. I think that the outrage of the citizenry there is growing, and will explode soon."

The MI6 operative was dubious. "How do we know that you aren't going to go report back to your handlers and tell them everything you learned about our operations?" He looked around the table at his colleagues, and spoke to them in English. "I think we should send him back to East Berlin. The Stasi can do with him what they want. They will probably just kill him, since he's of no further use to them now that his cover is blown."

The CIA agent protested. "Now wait a minute, there's no cause for that. This fella has got some info for us. Let's not throw it away. Let him talk."

Sergei understood English, and realized that he had to use all his oratorical skills to convince his interrogators of his *bona fides*. His fate was in their hands, and he had no power over them except the value of the information he could provide and his ability to make them believe it.

"I think that the government of Erich Honecker is on its last legs. It doesn't command the support of Moscow any more. With the advent of *perestroika* there, the Russians have no stomach for sending in the tanks to put down revolts in Eastern

Europe. If enough East Germans go out in the streets to protest, the regime could collapse."

"Tell us about the relations between the Stasi and the KGB," the West German BKA agent demanded.

"As is well known, the Russians want to destabilize Western Europe. The KGB finances terrorist groups like the Red Army Faction, and uses the Stasi as an intermediary since we are more knowledgeable about the situation in West Germany and can more easily operate there undetected. The Russian agents stick out like a sore thumb!" He laughed derisively.

"So you have dealt with the KGB?"

"Of course. We don't do any espionage work abroad without consulting them. At home it's a different story. We're much better than the KGB in keeping track of any opposition to the regime through a network of informants. We're aware of any hint of criticism of the government, and make sure that it's punished."

"Is it true that the Stasi has ordered assassinations of opponents to the regime?" the CIA man asked.

"Yes, it's true. I was not involved."

The CIA agent looked at his colleagues, who seemed unconvinced by Sergei's denial.

The woman attached to MI6 passed the agent a note. After glancing at it, he asked: "How do you see a protest against the regime playing out? After all, whenever they occurred in the past, including in 1956 or 1968, protests just led to more repression and the imprisonment of those opposing the regime."

"What's different now is that the gap between the West and the East is so blatantly obvious. People are so much richer in the West, can access so many more goods, and have greater freedom to do what they want. It's increasingly evident to those in the East since communication between the two sides, even if censored by Communist regimes, is far greater than before, given the advances in technology. I don't think Honecker has the stomach for it anymore. Even the Russians are getting tired of the Cold War!"

"We'll want to talk to you again," the MI6 agent said. "You'll be interned here on the base." Sergei was led away by a uniformed British army officer.

Lahr, Germany, March 1991

"We're going to need to wind down our joint operation. Now that Germany is one country again and the Iron Curtain is no more, a lot of Canadian and British forces are going to be sent home. I'm heading back to Canada myself in a month; my tour of duty is over. We've got to destroy all the paperwork. We can't let them discover the common invoices we've been sending to both of our employers."

"Right-o. What are you going to do when you go back to wearing civvies?"

"What do you think? I'll get a job in a restaurant–that's the only trade I know."

"I may follow you back over there to Canada. I don't fancy going back to Old Blighty. I just want to get demobbed and leave Britain. In the meantime, they're giving me a sendoff here at HQ–a gala dinner to mark the end of my days here as the head of procurement. I think my CO will miss the gourmet foods I've managed to put on his table!"

2

When the man heard the crickets starting to chirp he figured that it was dusk. Wearing black neoprene gloves, he opened the side door of his white panel truck a crack to confirm, then gathered up his equipment. He had parked on the street in front of an unoccupied house where a renovation was in progress. No one would be surprised to see another tradesman's vehicle there. It wasn't unusual for trucks to be left overnight, when they contained equipment and materials that were a nuisance to shuttle back and forth. He had waited patiently for nightfall in the truck's closed cargo bed, reading a crime novel by the illumination from the truck's dome light.

Carrying a black and yellow Dewalt tool bag, he got out of the truck and quickly walked the sidewalk to a mansion that was two houses away. Turning onto the lawn, he followed the hedge along the side of the property to avoid leaving footprints in the flowerbeds. Skirting the front entrance, he made for a door at the side of the house that was under an entrance roof. He first tried unsuccessfully to jimmy the door using a thin strip of Lexan plastic, then dug into his tool bag for his lock picks. In another minute he was inside the house.

He turned on his hockey-puck LED work light and looked around. The house was laid out as he had been told in his instructions. A door along the entrance hall led to a room that looked like it had once been a dining room, and was now an office. The grey steel filing cabinet was in the corner. It was locked, but the mechanism was so simple he could have picked it in the dark.

He leafed through the folders in the top drawer, looking for a particular name on the tab. When he found it, he removed the contents of the folder and stuck the half-dozen loose pages into his tool bag. He replaced the file folder, relocked the cabinet, and prepared to leave.

Turning toward the door, he started. A pair of yellow eyes were staring in his direction. No sound or motion had warned him of its approach. He froze, wondering if he should make a run for it. Trying to stay calm, he shone his work light in that direction, revealing a black furry animal. *Phew*, he thought, *it's only a cat.* It hissed at him but he ignored it, letting himself out and locking the entrance door behind him.

He returned to the panel truck and drove back to Halifax. After abandoning the stolen vehicle behind a warehouse, he walked the two kilometres back to his lodging in the North End, carrying his bag.

3

Hamish Cameron and Sean Carroll returned to The Oaks after an evening concert in a nearby park in Ashcroft-by-the-Sea, accompanied by Sean's companion, Marjoree Price. Marjoree lived in a townhouse not far away. The Oaks, Sean Carroll's ancestral home, was a mansion that exhibited its nineteenth century pedigree like a *grande dame* but was a bitch to maintain and required perpetual repairs. It was located in a cluster of imposing homes built when the town was a hub for shipping and a source of construction materials on Nova Scotia's South Shore, some fifty kilometres southwest of Halifax along Mahone Bay. The Oaks was where Hamish and Sean lived, and it also housed the detective agency, Cameron and Carroll, Investigators.

The concert was given by one of the Canadian groups that had been popular in the 1980s, and was still living off its glory days, replaying their hits rather than composing new music. They played in a bandshell while the audience either stood or sat on the grass. It was one of those fragrant June evenings, when the scent of the flowers and the warm air combined to signal that summer was near.

"I didn't think the tenor sax player was much good, did you?" Marjoree said. "I don't know if he was in the original band or was just a stand-in. But it was a nice evening. Couldn't have asked for better weather. And it was great hearing those old tunes again." Marjoree, a strawberry blond widow, usually saw the bright side of things.

Sean nodded his head. "Probably a replacement for one of the original members of the band. He's much younger than the others. They're certainly getting on in years." He chuckled. "Us too!" Sean was in his late forties, a decade younger than Marjorie, and much younger than Hamish.

This unlikely threesome met when Hamish and Marjoree had been residents of an upscale retirement home, New Dawn, in Ashcroft-by-the-Sea, and Sean was a volunteer there. Hamish had become suspicious about the activities of those who ran New Dawn, in particular requiring the residents to take a slew of multi-coloured pills each day. When his friend, John Devlin, died, Hamish was determined to investigate, and he enlisted Sean to help him. A series of events culminated in arson that levelled the residence and put its occupants onto the street. Sean was able to house Hamish in his ramshackle mansion, while Marjoree bought a new townhouse which had just been built nearby. Sean and Hamish continued their sleuthing in response to requests from locals who had learned about their success in investigating New Dawn. Ultimately, they decided to go into business together and founded Cameron and Carroll, Investigators. Marjoree and Sean had become close friends in the meantime, and she volunteered to help run the detective agency.

Hamish went out to the kitchen and came back holding a bottle of Prosecco and three glasses. "Let's have some bubbly to close out the evening! There's nothing on my schedule for to-morrow, except to go through some old trial notes that I made when I was still a judge." Hamish had retired a few years before at age 75, as required by Nova Scotia's statutes. "I've been hired by a friend of mine, Des Stuart, who owns a restaurant in down-town Halifax. I used to go there fairly often when I was still on the bench, since it was near to my chambers on Upper Water Street. He wants us to find out information on someone he says is trying to drive him out of business. It turns out it's a fellow who came before my court on charges of fraud concerning the alcohol that was served at his restaurant."

Sean scratched his chin. "So we're getting involved in indus-trial espionage?"

"No, I made it very clear to Des that there are some lines we will not cross; in particular, we wouldn't do anything illegal like breaking into someone's home or place of business to get infor-mation. The person's name is Serge Dimanche. He owns a chain of restaurants, and he lives not far from here, on a waterfront estate in Chester."

"He's the fellow who started the BistroDimanche franchise, isn't he? It's quite popular now, there must be at least three or four of those restaurants here in the province. It serves French bistro food. I've been to the Halifax restaurant a few times."

Hamish popped the cork and poured out three glasses, giving the first one to Marjoree. He smiled at her. "I'm glad you agreed to help out here at the detective agency, answering phones and keeping track of client information. But life's not all work and no play! Has Sean at least got you back into sailing? I know he still does the Wednesday night races at the yacht club." Sean was a lifelong sailor. He was a member of the Ashcroft Yacht Club, which was located only a short walk away from his house.

Before she could reply, Sean's black short-hair cat, Stanfield, came into the room and rubbed insistently against his legs.

Sean petted the cat. "I fed him before we left for the concert. Don't tell me he's hungry again!"

When Sean got up to go to the kitchen, where Stanfield's bowl was located, the cat instead went toward the detective agency's office, which was located in what had once been a large dining room. He jumped on top of the file cabinet, and started meowing.

Sean laughed and called to the others: "I think he wants to tell us something! Apparently he's not asking for food. But why should he be interested in the file cabinet?"

He searched for the key, which was in a drawer of a mahogany desk that was nearby. Hamish and Marjoree had come into the room, and they watched him open the cabinet. "I can't see what Stanfield is going on about," Sean said.

Hamish shrugged his shoulders. "Well, I might as well get out my notes on Serge Dimanche's trial." Pulling out the folder with that name on it, he looked up in surprise. "There's nothing in it! What happened to them? I'm sure my trial notes were in here."

4

"There's no evidence of anyone breaking and entering the house. I don't know when the file cabinet was burgled, though. It could have been months ago. There's no way of seeing if there's something in a file unless you take it out, and I haven't looked at those notes since I retired."

Hamish was talking to Sean the next morning in the detective agency office. They had searched for any clues as to why the notes were missing. No other files seemed to have disappeared. There were some antique candlesticks on the fireplace mantle, and a desktop computer with a flat screen monitor, which were also untouched.

Sean scratched his head. "I suppose if one of us had left the cabinet unlocked, or with the key in the lock, a nosy person might have looked in there at some point. But why take that file and not others? And I'm not aware of anyone being in the house recently, except the regular cleaners. I think it can only be the doing of a burglar who was specially looking for the Dimanche file. But why? What was in that file?"

"As I told you yesterday, I tried him for fraud involving the liquor he sold in his restaurants. Though I don't remember details, the whole case centred on the testimony of one witness, who had worked for Dimanche but had since left his employ. He was expected to testify that Dimanche's restaurants served contraband wine and liquor that was advertised as the real thing, and that he had been raking in money illegally for years. But the witness never showed up in court. The Halifax Regional Police and the RCMP looked for him, but they never found a trace. Of course, Dimanche was suspected of foul play, but they never found any proof of that. So he was let off. My notes probably included the witness's name and details of the search for him, as well as some background on Serge Dimanche."

"That doesn't sound important enough to justify burglary, especially not five years after the fact!"

"I wish I could remember what was in the file; my memory isn't what it was, and some of the other body parts don't work as well as they should either!" Hamish laughed. "This what I feel like reciting when someone says that age is just a number:

My sight is growing dimmer;

My mind is getting dumber;

My feet are feeling numb;

Isn't old age a bummer?!"

Sean shook his head. "You're doing fine, Hamish. You're sharp as a tack. In any case, won't the trial records have all that information? Why should someone steal your notes?"

"I can get someone to dig out the court's trial records for me, but there must be something more in my notes that's important. First thing to do, we have to report the burglary to the police, and you'd better install some better locks on the outside doors and the file cabinet. Then I'll try to find out why this happened.

I'm going to poke around to see whether I can learn more about Dimanche–assuming he's involved in this one way or another."

"I'll see what I can find out about him online." Sean had a background in IT, having been the Internet specialist for a large corporation in the US before he took early retirement. "There's a lot of personal information in public databases and on social media. That's where I would start."

*****

Joe Washington, a black Nova Scotian who was the RCMP Commander for the Lunenburg district, was accompanied by one of his constables. They were responding to the complaint of a burglary at The Oaks. Decades before, Joe had been a classmate of Sean's at Ashcroft's Riverview High School. He was broad shouldered and fit looking, not having turned into an overweight version of his former self like many at his age who had been football players in high school and college. He gave Sean a friendly jab in the shoulder and shook Hamish's hand.

"So when did you discover the burglary? What's missing?"

"That's the problem," Hamish responded. "We don't know when it happened–except that Sean's cat led us to the filing cabinet so we're guessing it occurred when we were away last evening. What was taken has no monetary value. It would seem to be of use only to the individual who appeared before my court a number of years ago, or to someone with an interest in his case." Hamish went on to explain the circumstances of Dimanche's trial, repeating what he had told Sean. "I don't have any clues or evidence of a break-in, but I felt it had to be reported to the police."

"Very well, I'll make note of it. I'll have my constable look for evidence that someone might have recently entered your house illegally. We'll open a case file, but unless we find something here I don't think you can expect this to go anywhere."

The constable looked around the office and at the entrance doors but there was no evidence of locks being forced. A brief search of the grounds turned up nothing. Their job done, the two RCMP officers went back to the Lunenburg district office on Lilydale Road.

5

"Sean, the trial records give the name of the witness who was called to testify but never did, a certain Seamus Dooley, with an address in Dartmouth. This was five years ago, but, who knows, I might just find someone in the Portland Hills neighbourhood of Dartmouth where he lived who remembers him." Hamish had packed an overnight bag, planning to stay with his friend Izzie French in Halifax after looking around Dartmouth. She taught securities law at Dalhousie, and lived in an apartment near the university. "Have you managed to get a locksmith to come in?"

"The side entrance door should have a new lock by the time you get back. Better call first to be sure someone will be around to let you in. Before you go, here's what I found out about Serge Dimanche on the Internet. The corporate website for BistroDimanche says that he founded his first restaurant on Halifax's Upper Water Street in 1997. Given its enormous success–their phrase–he opened another one in Sydney the year after. Then he created a corporate structure and franchised two new restaurants, in New Glasgow and Bridgewater."

"Interesting. Does it say anything about Serge Dimanche's background? Where he came from?"

"His bio on the website talks about growing up in Provence and learning to cook traditional French food from home-grown ingredients, but doesn't give other details. Nor does it mention any work experience at restaurants in Europe. A search for 'Serge Dimanche' yields nothing until the late 1990s, when his restaurants started being mentioned in the Chronicle-Herald's business section and his presence at fund-raising galas reported on their society pages. A more recent article mentions problems with the restaurant chain's finances, partly due to Covid-19, but also because the newer BistroDimanche restaurants are in smaller towns which don't see much tourism or demand for French food."

"So maybe his financial difficulties are leading him to go head-to-head with his nearest competitor. After all, Desmond Stuart's restaurant is only a few blocks away from Halifax's BistroDimanche."

*****

Hamish drove his almost new Prius up Highway 103 into Halifax, down North Street, and across the Macdonald Bridge into Dartmouth. He marvelled at the vista from the bridge, under which a large freighter was passing on its way out to the ocean. On the other side he wound his way through downtown Dartmouth and found his way to Portland Hills.

Hamish rang the bell of a modest bungalow on a quiet street where Seamus Dooley used to live. He didn't have much hope of finding anyone home, so he wasn't too surprised when no one answered the bell. He looked at the houses on either side. They were close together on small lots so the neighbours probably all knew each other.

He tried the right-hand-side house. A middle-aged woman with a scarf around her hair came to the entrance. The sound of a television soap opera filtered outside. She held the door open about a foot, looking questioningly at Hamish. "Yes?"

"I'm trying to track down a man who lived next door, Seamus Dooley. I know it's been a long time since he lived there, but do you know anything about him?"

"Yes, I remember Seamus. What's your interest?"

"He was supposed to testify at my court five years ago, but never showed. Something happened recently to make me want to try to find him again." He gave her the card for Cameron and Carroll, Investigators. "I'm Hamish Cameron."

"So, you're a detective as well as a judge?" She looked at him sceptically.

"Former judge. I retired at 75." He laughed. "I know I don't look it, but it's true!"

The woman smiled, and looked somewhat reassured. "OK, here's what little I know. I haven't seen him since he disappeared five years ago. A few days later, two guys came to his house and took all his stuff and put it into a pickup truck. There wasn't much. I tried to chat up the movers, but they wouldn't say where they were taking his junk nor where he might be. The house displayed a 'for rent' sign a few days later and it's been occupied by a young couple for the last five years. End of story."

"Did he have family around here? Anybody else in the neighbourhood who might know where he is?"

"Why don't you try the restaurant in Halifax? The house on the other side has tenants who've only been there a year."

"OK, thanks. Keep my card, and if anything occurs to you, give me a call." Hamish gave her a quick nod and headed back to his car. He turned. "What's the address of the restaurant?"

"I don't know the number, it's one of those near the harbour, on Upper Water Street. It's called BistroDimanche."

*****

The restaurant was decorated like a Paris bistro, with darkly varnished wooden panels and marble facing on the dining room walls. There were a few tables with red and white checked tablecloths on the sidewalk. A bar with a zinc countertop ran alongside one of the walls of the dining room. The restaurant was retro and stylish rather than fancy.

The time was just five o'clock and all the tables were empty, but two men sat at the bar talking loudly and sipping glasses of wine, and another man was on a stool further down, nursing a beer.

Hamish walked up to the end of the bar, away from the other patrons, and beckoned the bartender over. He was a man in his late twenties or early thirties, and Hamish thought he might be too new to have known Dooley. "I'm looking for a former employee. Is there a manager here I can talk to?"

"You're in luck, he just came in to get the place ready for dinner time." He picked up the phone. "There's a man here to see you."

A burly man in his forties emerged from a hall at the end of the dining room, which Hamish assumed led to the kitchen and the manager's office. He was dressed in a well-worn black suit, a dress shirt, and no tie. His face showed preoccupation with the demands of his job. He looked warily at Hamish. "What can I do for you?"

"I'm looking for a former employee, Seamus Dooley who worked here before—over five years ago. I realize that's quite far in the past, but maybe you can give me a clue to his whereabouts now?"

"Who wants to know?"

Hamish gave him his card. He resorted to a white lie: "I've been hired by the estate of a relative to find him. He's been left some money."

"He was the manager and chef before me. I never met him, but I heard he left in a hurry. I was hired to take his place, and I've been here for the last five years."

"You don't have a forwarding address for Dooley? The restaurant must have filed some paperwork, withheld taxes for him, and so forth."

"If the company did, it wasn't done here. We don't keep personnel files. This place is part of a chain, and most of the administrative stuff is done at head office. I hire the wait staff and order food, but the menu is set by the head office and they manage the payroll."

"And the head office is where?"

"In Bridgewater. The owner lives not far from there, on Mahone Bay."

"How do I get in touch with him?"

"He wants any inquiries to go through head office." He gave Hamish a card with the contact details. He looked toward the kitchen. "I've got things to do. Sorry I can't be of more help." He turned and walked away, leaving Hamish standing there.

As Hamish was leaving the man sitting alone motioned to him, so he ambled over to the bar, looking inquiringly at the fellow, who was casually dressed and middle-aged. Hamish guessed that he was retired, and this was his regular watering hole.

"I heard you asking about Seamus Dooley. I knew the guy pretty well, he worked here for a number of years before he had a falling out with the boss, Serge Dimanche. He quit his job, or got fired–I don't know which. Soon after, he moved out of his house in Dartmouth and disappeared. It happened suddenly and I never got a chance to talk to him again. If anyone would know where he went, it would be Dimanche himself."

Hamish nodded. "I came to that conclusion too, but I don't know that he'll talk to me." He shrugged. "It's worth a try, though. Do you know why they had a falling out?"

He looked around before answering in a near whisper. "Seamus thought the guy was sailing too close to the wind, if you get my drift. But I suspect that my friend might also have been skimming off the top. I heard Dimanche accuse him of ripping off some of the food to sell to another restaurant. For whatever reason, they were not on good terms when he left."

6

Hamish and Izzie were having left-over eggplant lasagna in her apartment, accompanied by a bottle of Nero d'Avola. Hamish gave a contented sigh. "I'm stuffed, but I'll take another sip of this nice wine." He stretched out his legs and looked around the room, admiring, not for the first time, the Pirandello prints on the wall and the Isfahan carpet on the floor of the dining room. Her flat, though not large, was perfect for her needs, well situated, and tastefully furnished.

Hamish and Izzie had known each other for decades, since the time they were junior lawyers at different Halifax legal firms. They had been on opposite sides of a suit involving the disappearance of a diamond necklace. Hamish had been given the task of defending the jeweller, who had agreed to store the necklace in his safe, against the accusation of negligence by his insurance company, which refused to compensate the owner of the necklace for her loss. Izzie was suspicious of the necklace owner's actions, and she passed them on surreptitiously to Hamish. She realized that her firm's client, the insurance company, would benefit from shifting the focus away from the jeweller and onto the owner herself, though they could not attack her directly. In the end, the court absolved the jeweller and tried the woman for fraud. Hamish came out a hero in the eyes of his firm.

Izzie started to clear the table of dishes. "How did your visit to BistroDimanche go? I've been there once, and wasn't too thrilled by the food. It's OK, but it's more like a Mcdonalds serving French food than a Michelin-starred restaurant."

"All right, I guess. I didn't get any clues concerning Dooley's whereabouts, but I did learn that he seems to have left the restaurant by mutual consent with his boss, since they disagreed about a number of things. By the way, how about coming with me to the UNICEF Water for Life Gala here in Halifax? They have some good local chefs serving foods from around the world, and Serge Dimanche will be there. He'll be showcasing some of his French bistro food."

"When is it?"

"It's coming up next week. It will cost us a bundle, of course—these charity events always do. I know you don't think much of his food, but at least it will give me a chance to meet Serge Dimanche."

"That's OK with me, it's for a good cause, and it'll give us a chance to sample some other cuisines. Plus, we can walk there from here. We won't want to be driving, not if we also enjoy the wines throughout the evening!" Izzie's apartment was near the Dalhousie University campus, a short walk up the hill from the Convention Centre where the gala was to be held.

*****

Hamish was wearing an evening jacket with black tie, and Izzie a full-length blue gown that showed off her still attractive figure, despite being roughly the same age as Hamish. He had a distinguished look as befitted a judge, and her high cheekbones and lean face suggested a former movie star or model. They made a handsome couple.

Half of the room at the Convention Centre was devoted to tables serving buffet food, and the other half to tables seating the diners. Banners behind each of the serving stations indicated the name of the restaurant and its cuisine. Dimanche was standing behind a table containing an assortment of his French bistro food, kept warm in chafing dishes heated by alcohol lamps–*steak-frites, saumon à l'oseille, bœuf Bourguignon, and petit salé au lentilles*–as well as some desserts on platters–*île flottante* and *crème brûlée*, among others. Wearing his chef's toque and white apron, his bulk proving that he enjoyed eating as well as cooking, he seemed the archetypical genial French restaurateur. His large face sported a broad smile, as he served the dishes to those of the diners who strolled by who wanted to sample his offerings. The sign behind him on the wall proudly showcased the chain's Halifax restaurant with a street view and a photo of the dining room inside.

Hamish and Izzie stopped by a few of the other restaurant tables, then ambled over to the one for BistroDimanche. Making eye-contact with Dimanche, Hamish asked him about the *petit salé aux lentilles*: "Isn't that a bit unfamiliar to North Americans? A stew made with salt pork and lentils?"

"Yes, you're right, but as soon as they try it they see how good it is! It's one of our most popular dishes. At home we ate it at least one Sunday a month."

"Do you still take a hand in the cooking, or leave it to others?"

"Only very occasionally, for gala occasions like this, or a special dinner at one of my local restaurants. I enjoy cooking, but mostly just do it for my family and friends now."

Dimanche agreed to pose with Hamish, and Izzie took their picture with her smartphone.

"I imagine the restaurants pretty much run themselves, don't they?" Hamish continued. You don't need to be hands-on any more."

"That's true, though I'm in constant touch with my head office in Bridgewater and involved in any major decision."

"Like playing tricks on the competition?" Hamish looked at him sternly.

Dimanche's smile turned into a frown, and he glared at Hamish. "What do you mean by that? And who sent you? You're from the press, aren't you?"

Hamish glared back. "You don't remember me? I'm the judge who tried the case against you for fraud."

"How dare you harass me at a charity event? I was exonerated at the trial."

Hamish ignored this, and continued: "The Crown's key witness disappeared before he could testify. What happened to him?"

Dimanche was sullen now, his anger in check and his voice kept low. "I don't know. I had no contact with him after he stopped working for me. Now please leave me alone." He turned to greet another patron with a forced smile. "The best French food this side of Finisterre!"

When they got back to their table with their plates, Izzie commented: "Well, that didn't go well. You could have tried to sweet talk him, rather than accuse him directly. You can catch more flies with honey than vinegar! So what do you do now?"

"Sean and I will have to look into his background and try to talk to his confederates. There must be some link between the burglary and Dimanche himself. I wonder how he knew that I was investigating him? Could our phones be bugged?"

"More likely it's your friend Des in the restaurant business whose phones are bugged. Especially since he thinks that Dimanche is using dirty tricks against him."

"That makes sense. By the way, now I remember one of the things I jotted down in my notes at the trial five years ago. The Queen's Counsel, a francophone, told me that he overheard Serge Dimanche talking to one of his lawyers in French and his accent was a bit off–neither Provençal nor Parisian. So his story of growing up in France and learning how to cook in his grandmother's kitchen in Provence doesn't ring true."

7

Desmond

Before heading back to Ashcroft, Hamish stopped at the elegant French restaurant on Lower Water Street in Halifax, *Bord de l'eau,* that Desmond Stuart owned. Hamish had frequented the restaurant when he was a judge and had his chambers nearby. After a while the two had become friends. Desmond was a sociable fellow, and he enjoyed hearing from Hamish about what went on in court.

The decals in the window next to the entrance door indicated that *Bord de l'eau* was a TripAdvisor top pick and part of the French *Relais et Châteaux* chain of gourmet restaurants and boutique hotels. *A cut above BistroDimanche,* Hamish reminded himself. It was too early for dinner so the door was locked. Hamish rang the bell.

Desmond Stuart was a large gentleman with a florid face and traces of his native Scottish brogue in his speech. He greeted

Hamish warmly in the doorway and ushered him into the intimate dining room, which was decorated with Art Nouveau posters and old photos of Paris buildings and monuments. Staff were setting the tables with white cloths, silverware, and an array of wine glasses. Discreet lighting was provided by lamps on each table, giving the room an air of romance.

"We're missing one of our waiters. He left without giving notice–that damned fellow Dimanche hired him away. We'll have to make do with only two. Fortunately my chef is true blue–he'll stick with me even if Dimanche offers him twice his salary! Anyway, he knows that here he can be inventive, not just be a cog in the corporate machine that serves up tired old recipes that anyone who has lived in France has eaten *ad nauseam.*"

"Des, why do you think that Dimanche has it in for you? His bistro food is no match for your gourmet cuisine."

"That's a good question. I guess it's because we show him up as being second rate. Perhaps he aspires to be *the* French restaurant in Halifax. To be honest, many of the tourists who patronize his outlets wouldn't know the difference. But he resents the fact that there are people of taste in this town who do, and wouldn't be seen dead in BistroDimanche! I also hear that his restaurants are in trouble. If he can put me out of business, he may hope that some of my clientele will migrate over to his bistro. Fat chance of that!"

"Anyway, I stopped by to tell you about my progress, or rather lack of it, in finding out useful information on Serge Dimanche. I tried to find the fellow who was supposed to testify at his trial, but got nowhere beyond locating two individuals who knew him: a neighbour in Dartmouth and a patron of the restaurant. Neither had any idea what happened to him, though–he just disappeared. I'll keep digging. I should warn you that your phone might be bugged. Some notes I made at the trial seem to have been stolen, so someone must have discovered that you hired me, and why."

"Oh, Christ, I should have known. How about we communicate using WhatsApp? That should be relatively secure, given that messages are encrypted end-to-end."

"Fine. By the way, I went to the UNICEF Gala and actually talked to Dimanche. I told him that I was looking for Seamus Dooley, the witness who disappeared. That made him angry, but he didn't give anything away."

"Be careful, Hamish. I think Dimanche is ruthless. Don't provoke him needlessly."

"You should contact the police. They could patrol the area around your restaurant more frequently than they do now."

"I guess so. But I really don't have anything to prove to them that I'm under threat. There's been no actual physical violence, no break-in, no smashed windows. And I can't accuse Dimanche. He's a well-known member of the business community and a philanthropist to boot. No one would take me seriously."

8

The next day Desmond rang Hamish to complain that some-one was again playing dirty tricks on him. "There's a post on Twitter saying that my place is not a restaurant–it's a bordello! It's gone viral. Apparently a lot of people find amusing the play-on-words derived from the pronunciation of the restaurant's name, *Bord de l'eau.* I chose the name because we're on Water Street, hence the French phrase which means 'on the water.' I suspect Serge Dimanche is behind this slur but I have no proof. The person who posted the joke has the username @Foodfinder, but I don't know his true identity."

"I'll ask Sean to look into it for you. He may be able to identify the person involved."

*****

Sean was happy to search the net for the identity of the poster who claimed the restaurant was a bordello. "There are plenty of reverse-people-search tools, like IDCrawl and Social Catfish. First I'll just Google 'Foodfinder' to see what comes up." After a minute of scrolling down through the search results, he gave up. "Nothing useful here, except a lot of sites with that name that give recipes and locate restaurants serving various cuisines.

Now I'll input 'Foodfinder' into Social Catfish. They charge a fee to identify someone on social media, but if the search is successful it will come back with the person's aliases on various social media sites, his true name, and his contact info. While I'm at it, why don't you send me a copy of the photo that Izzie took of you and Serge Dimanche? I'll do a direct search by entering his name and photo into a facial recognition app like TruthFinder, which should be able to match them with his usernames on the social media sites. Doing both a direct and reverse search should turn up something. It'll take a few minutes, Hamish, to get some results."

The results were surprising. Serge Dimanche did not seem to have any presence on social media. A search of the Internet using facial imaging did find some recent newspaper photos that identified him, but these were the ones that Sean was already aware of. Nothing else came up. It was as if he had deliberately chosen not to be visible. The only contact information found for him was Info@BistroDimanche.com. As for the reverse search for 'Foodfinder,' it was unable to identify the person behind that alias.

Sean passed the information on to Hamish. "It looks as though Serge Dimanche has gone to extreme lengths to be invisible on the internet. I wonder why that is?"

"Maybe he's just not interested in using social media or in being able to communicate by email. Some of us old-timers just prefer privacy over self-advertisement. Either way, that makes him an unusual individual these days. What about trying to find Seamus Dooley?"

"It would help if we had a photo of him. If he disappeared of his own choice, then he's probably using a new name. Of course he also would want to remain under cover in that case, so I wouldn't hold out much hope of finding a match for his photo."

A search for "Seamus Dooley" turned up contact information for a number of them, including an actor, a journalist, and a player of Gaelic football, but no one offering a likely match with the former manager of the Halifax restaurant. The only reference to him was in an article in the Halifax Chronicle-Herald at the time of the trial that gave the name of the witness who had disappeared. Since then, nothing.

9

Sean and Hamish met at breakfast in the kitchen the next morning. The large room, which was next to the former dining room that served as the detective agency office at present, was well equipped with an ancient six-burner gas stove and plenty of counter and cabinet space, as well as room for an ample breakfast table that could seat six.

Sean yawned. "I'll be working on the insurance case all day. But if you need me to do more searching for info on Serge Dimanche, I can get to it tomorrow."

"Tell me again what this insurance case is all about."

"We've been hired to investigate an insurance claim by a Halifax food supply company that wants to be compensated for the theft of its products. Atlantic Food Services supplies produce, meat, and seafood to restaurants in Halifax and surrounding areas. Over the past few months, several restaurants have complained that they didn't receive some of the food they ordered. AFS pointed out that in each case it had left the company's warehouse, according to its automated inventory management system. The insurance company has refused to continue to pay compensation to AFS until an investigation is done into the source of the losses. We've been hired to do that."

*****

Sean was speaking to the manager of AFS's Dartmouth warehouse, an expansive one-story building in an industrial section of town. This was where the food that AFS purchased from wholesalers or directly from producers was stored until it could be delivered by refrigerated truck to restaurants and institutional clients such as hospitals or schools. "It's really quite simple," Arturo Goya said. "The food comes in, we barcode it, and it goes into our cold rooms. We keep a large inventory, so we can usually supply what our customers need. When an order is processed, we scan each item, put it into a box, which is sealed with tape and barcoded with the client's information. When the truck is loaded, each box gets scanned. We know exactly what we have in stock, we monitor when it comes in, and when it goes out. What happens when the truck leaves our warehouse I have no idea. That's a separate department, shipping. They deal with the logistics of delivering the food, keeping the trucks in operating condition, and garaging them. They're located in Bedford."

"So the orders come in to you directly?"

"No, they're received by staff at head office, either made on our website or phoned in, and they arrange to receive payment or charge the customer's account. Then they send us instructions for delivery."

Sean asked a few more questions, then drove over to Bedford, to the sprawling garages and parking lot of the Shipping Department, where AFS's refrigerated trucks in a range of sizes were to be found. The transportation coordinator there was equally dogmatic. "Each driver is issued with a barcode reader, and every pre-packed box that he or she delivers is scanned as it leaves the truck. The driver is responsible for the load and is under strict instructions not to leave the truck unattended. It is 100 percent certain that the box that left the warehouse for a particular order is the one that is delivered to the customer."

"What if the driver needs to go into a washroom, or stops at some place for coffee? Is the tailgate locked? And does the customer open the boxes in front of the driver, to verify that everything that was ordered is there?"

"The driver is supposed to put the padlock on the back door of the truck unless he or she keeps it in sight. In any case, it's a heavy door, since the truck is refrigerated, and not easily opened. No, the driver doesn't stick around to witness the restaurant open the boxes. That would take too much time. The driver needs to get going in order to make the next delivery. On average, a truck picks up 20 orders at the warehouse and delivers them all in a typical run of four to six hours. There just isn't time at each stop to open each box and check its contents."

"When do you learn from the restaurant that they didn't get their full order?"

"They call head office, which notifies the warehouse to send out another shipment. After they put it together, they call us to send a truck to make the delivery. If it was due to a shortfall in the original order, they'll let us know then."

"So, how much time is there typically between the first delivery and when you learn that there was a problem?"

"A day, sometimes longer."

"The delay in getting their full order must be a real problem for a restaurant, if they planned for a certain number of servings of a particular dish and find that they don't have enough food to make them all."

The man shrugged his shoulders. "Well, they just have to offer another menu item instead."

"Tell me, is it always the same restaurants that are short of some of the food they ordered? And is the driver the same?"

"I'd have to look, but I don't think so."

*****

Sean went to talk to the customer service manager at the head office of AFS, which was located near to the warehouse in Dartmouth but in a separate building. Jeff Winding was a paunchy fellow in his mid-forties, who was starting to go bald on top. He scratched his head in response to Sean's request for data on the shortfalls in delivery, then stopped suddenly after realizing what he was doing.

"I'll get Beth to look through our records. We haven't been keeping track–I guess we should have."

"Please make it a rush job. I can't make any progress on this until I know what we're dealing with. I'll need the names of the driver and the restaurant, its location, and the items that were missing."

*****

The data was contained in a spreadsheet attached to an email sent to the detective agency. Sean, back in the office, sat at his desk, a cup of coffee in his right hand, and peered at his computer's screen. The list of delivery shortfalls began five months before. There were eight entries, presented in rows that reported details of each incident.

Sean could not discern any particular pattern. Six drivers were involved, only two of whom made a defective delivery twice. The restaurants were also diverse, and their locations varied, though most were located in downtown Halifax. Sean imagined that this could be because that was the location of most of AFS's customers, but he made a note to check with Winding. He plotted the restaurants' location on Google Maps to see if there was any clustering. He thought: *I should have asked for the driver's route in each case. I'll do that too.*

The items missing were in each case fancy cuts of meat or fish, typically beef or salmon steaks, or lobster. *That's not surprising. They must be the high-value items.*

He considered the timing of the defective deliveries. They all occurred on different dates. *So only one shipment was affected each time, perhaps only one box. That might be significant.* He entered the dates on Google Calendar, and noted that in each case the defective delivery occurred on a Friday. *Perhaps this is because some restaurants typically do most of their business on the weekend. I'll find out if that's the busiest day for deliveries by AFS.*

Having done what he could to analyse the data he was given, he sent off a request to Winding for the further information he needed.

10

Des called Hamish again. "Now someone has splattered red paint on the front door of my restaurant! We've got to do something about this. I called the Halifax police, and they said they would make a point to check on my place occasionally, but they can't do that 24/7. Anyone can just saunter by with a can of paint and toss it while no one is looking!"

"You might want to install cameras on both sides of the front of your building, aimed toward the door in the centre, and put some at the back entrance too."

"OK, I'll do that, but they'll just find some other way to sabotage my restaurant! Just last week I didn't get a full order of food delivered to me. The food service said they didn't know how that happened, but it meant that I had to turn some customers away. They only delivered the rest of the order the next day."

"You think it was sabotage?"

"I don't know. At present, everything seems like sabotage to me. Can't you find some way to hit back at Serge Dimanche? I'm sure he's the one behind all that's been happening to me."

"As I told you, Des, our detective agency draws the line at anything illegal, including playing dirty tricks on competitors or threatening them. But I'll continue trying to find out things about Serge Dimanche and his restaurant, and report back to you."

*****

Hamish caught Sean back at the office with another request. "Would it be possible to do a search for Seamus Dooley using facial recognition apps? I managed to locate a photograph of him in the Chronicle-Herald, taken when the Halifax BistroDimanche first opened."

"I can try, though a newspaper photo is pretty low definition. Let's see what turns up."

After a few minutes of searching, the software came up with a dozen possible matches. Three were posted on social media, while the others were in newspaper or magazine archives. Sean scrolled through them.

Hamish looked over Sean's shoulder. "The first one is definitely not him. It's of a much younger man, even though the article where it appears is only a year old. Oh, there's one that looks like a match, and the photo was taken well before his disappearance." The photo was from a story about Nova Scotia restaurants from a travel magazine. It showed the chef posing in front of a building in Digby sporting the name "Scallops by the Bay." "Maybe that's where he worked before he took the job at BistroDimanche. I'll try contacting the place, assuming it's still in business. They might be able to fill in some details about his background. Let's keep going and look at the other photos."

The next few potential matches were photos from print articles that did not seem clear enough to make a judgement concerning the individual's identity, nor did the stories provide any useful information about the person portrayed. However, one of the photos found on a Facebook page seemed a plausible match. It showed a man beside a younger woman, with the caption "Me and my father at the Reversing Falls." The poster's name was given as Mary Carstairs, and the date was two years ago.

Hamish was excited. "This suggests that Seamus Dooley is alive, anyway. And if we can locate the right Mary Carstairs, presumably née Dooley, we may be able to find him. If he worked at that Digby restaurant, he may be from the Bay of Fundy area, and it could be that's where he went back to."

"The Facebook page doesn't give much information about her, just saying that she lives in Saint John, New Brunswick. But I can always message her to ask about her father."

"Be careful! You may just scare him away. I would do some more digging before trying to contact her."

"The Yellow Pages website lists two Mary Carstairs in Saint John. I'll print out their names and addresses. Let's see if they have a Seamus Dooley there too … No, not in the city. Anyway, there's no reason to believe that he lives with his daughter or that he's still using his real name."

"I'm going to pay a visit to Saint John, but first I'll make a stop in Digby, ask about Dooley at the restaurant there, and take the ferry across the Bay of Fundy. It'll be a pleasant trip, even if I don't find the fellow. Want to come?"

"I can't, I have to keep working on the AFS case. I've been trying to find a pattern in the thefts, so I'm poring through the data they've sent me. They promised to give me further information about what was stolen and the routes their drivers took. I hope to find a clue as to who might have done them."

11

Hamish followed Highway 103 to Trunk 8, which he took northwestward. This scenic road crossed mostly wooded and lightly populated areas, ran along the Mersey River in several places and after about 100 kilometres reached Annapolis Royal. From there, the Evangeline Trail, so named because of the famous poem by Longfellow about the deportation of Acadians in the mid 18th century, brought him to the outskirts of Digby. Settled by United Empire Loyalists following the American Revolution, it was a picturesque fishing and tourism centre on the sheltered Annapolis Basin, with access to the Bay of Fundy through a deepwater passage, the Digby Gut. He followed the road into town to the Scallops by the Bay restaurant.

Digby was a busy place during tourist season, as Hamish discovered when arriving in mid-morning. The small car park was full, and most of the parking spaces along the street where it was located were taken. He did find a spot eventually but had to walk back two blocks to the restaurant. He had time for only a quick bite before taking the Digby-Saint John ferry, which departed from a dock a few kilometres north of the town.

The quaint restaurant was housed in a 19th century wooden building, which was surrounded by rose bushes. They emitted a pleasant scent which combined with the that of seafood simmering in butter sauce provided an aromatic enticement to diners. The inside dining room was packed. Hamish noticed that there was a terrace at the back with a number of tables with parasols, overlooking the water and giving a view of the fishing fleet. It was full except for a small table near the rear entrance to the building. Hamish grabbed that spot and scanned the menu. He decided on a lobster sandwich.

A waitress dressed in a white uniform came over to take his order. She looked to be in her fifties, so Hamish guessed that she might have been at the restaurant during Dooley's tenure . "Tell me, do you remember Seamus Dooley, who was a chef here several years ago?"

"Seamus Dooley, you say? Oh, right, I do remember him. He was an OK guy to work for. Did you know him?"

"I just wondered what happened to him. Does he still live around here?"

"No, he moved away. He had a falling out with the owner here and quit. I understand he got a better paying job in Halifax. Haven't heard anything about him since."

"What do you mean by a falling out?"

"Seamus wanted a greater say in the menu and in procurement of provisions. The owner said no."

"I see. So he found greener pastures in Halifax."

"So I gather."

Hamish gobbled down his sandwich, paid the bill, and drove his car to join the queue waiting to board the ferry. After parking his car in the cargo hold as instructed by the intendants Hamish walked up to the top deck. The weather had turned bright and sunny, though a breeze off the water made it chilly. He stayed inside the cabin during the two hour trip across the Bay of Fundy, enjoying the views of the green tree-covered hills of New Brunswick as they approached their destination.

In Saint John, the address of the first Mary Carstairs on his list was a stone-faced apartment building four stories high in an old part of town near the city centre. He found her name on a mailbox and rang her bell, but got no answer. He rang the apartment's superintendent, who buzzed him in. Looking around the lobby, he saw a small office with its door wide open. Inside was a middle-aged man wearing blue overalls and with a set of keys on his belt. He nodded when Hamish entered and looked at him expectantly.

"Hi, I'm looking for Mary Carstairs, but since she didn't answer her bell, I'm guessing she's at work."

"Probably. You have business with her?"

Hamish fell back on his usual excuse: "She stands to inherit some money. Can you just tell me if she is the woman in this photograph?" He pulled out the picture of her and her father that had been posted on Facebook.

"Yes, that's Mary all right. If you want to leave me your card, I'll tell her to get in touch with you."

Hamish pulled out the detective agency's card with his cell phone number on it and handed it to him. He added: "You don't know where her father lives, by any chance?"

"I met him once when he was visiting Mary. I think he lives in Rothesay, but I couldn't tell you where. I do remember him saying that he was a chef in one of the restaurants there."

*****

Traffic through downtown Saint John was slow because of construction, but once he got onto Route 1 heading north, he was able to make good time. Nevertheless, it was past 5 o'clock when he got to Rothesay. Hamish discovered using Google Maps that most of the restaurants there were along Hampton Road. *I expect he'll have a job in one of the more upscale establishments, given his experience.*

He picked out three which seemed the likeliest possibilities, two Italian restaurants and a highly rated gastropub. The first one of these along Hampton Road was one of the Italian ones, a pizzeria. *This doesn't seem to fit with Dooley's background.* Hamish didn't bother to go in. The next one was the Beer Wagon Gastropub, easily spotted because of a large painting of a horse-drawn wagon filled with beer kegs. The restaurant was lodged in a replica of an English pub, complete with frosted glass windows and decorative wooden beams. *This looks more promising.*

The bar was crowded and most of the chairs in the dining area were occupied. Tables were laden with pitchers of beer and platters of appetising food. The patrons were talking animatedly so the noise level was high. Hamish had to wait a few minutes at the bar before the bartender came over to take his order. Speaking in a loud voice to make himself heard, Hamish asked him: "I'm looking for Seamus Dooley. I was told he might be the chef here."

The bartender shook his head. "Sorry, there's no one of that name here." He turned away.

"Wait, let me show you his picture." He pulled out the photo taken of him and his daughter. "Is this your chef?"

The bartender stared at it for a moment. "Nope, never saw that man in my life. Now, do you want to order? If not, I suggest you make room for actual customers." Two men were standing behind Hamish waiting to be served. He shrugged his shoulders, then pushed by them and left.

Back in the parking lot Hamish looked around for another entrance to the restaurant. *I don't think he was telling the truth. He hesitated a little too long before replying. If I can get into the kitchen I can check for myself.*

Walking around to the back, he noticed a windowless door with a sign saying Staff Only. A black Ford F-150 pickup was parked in front of it. The door to the building was unlocked and Hamish cautiously stepped inside. A hallway led past a storeroom to another door at the end. Hamish could hear chopping noises and the sizzling of food being fried. Opening the door a crack, he felt a wave of greasy air sweep over him. He could see that the kitchen was occupied by two people, a man with his back to him stirring a pan that was heating on the cooktop and a young woman chopping vegetables on a wooden counter. She looked up, and, seeing Hamish, said something to the chef. He turned around and motioned to Hamish to leave. "This is off limits to customers. Staff only!"

Hamish could see right away that the man was the person in the photograph. Instead of leaving as he was told, he advanced into the kitchen.

The chef became agitated. "If you don't leave now, I'll call the police!"

Hamish raised his hand, palm extended. "I wouldn't do that, if I were you, Seamus Dooley. You were supposed to testify in a court case five years ago and disappeared. If you call the police, I'll tell them who you really are, and you'll end up in jail."

"Who are you?" The man picked up a knife from the counter. "And what do you want?"

"My name is Hamish Cameron. I'm a detective looking into the affairs of Serge Dimanche. I'd like you to tell me what you know about him, and why you skipped out five years ago."

"You with the police?"

"No, I was hired by another restaurant owner who thinks Serge Dimanche is trying to sabotage his business. I need you to fill in some of the background."

"Oh yeah? And who might that be?"

"The restaurant's name is *Bord de l'eau.* It's owned by Desmond Stuart."

Dooley frowned, but put the knife down. "OK, I'll talk to you. But not now. I've got food to prepare, and it will be nonstop here for the next two hours. I can arrange to meet you after that."

"Is that your F-150 out back? Give me the keys. I'll be at a table in the dining room out front at eight o'clock. If you don't show, I'll call the police."

12

While he waited to have a late dinner at the Gastropub, Hamish checked into a motel down the street, and then went for a walk along the Kennebecasis River. He admired its wide expanse, dotted with anchored sailboats. He returned to the pub at 7:30 and ordered a dinner of fish and chips, accompanied by a pint of the local India Pale Ale. As he was finishing his deep-fried haddock Seamus Dooley came out from the kitchen, looked around, and came over to sit at Hamish's table.

"How did you find me? I've been using an assumed name."

"Through your daughter's Facebook post of a photo of you and her, which turned up when we searched for a facial match. So how did you get a driver's licence? I assume you have one, since you drive a truck. Before I forget, here are your keys."

"I grew up around Saint John, so I know people here. A friend of mine's brother by the name of Kevin Martin died in a farming accident. He was run over by a thresher. When I left Halifax to come back here, I took his identity. We were the same age, and we looked similar enough that the photo on his driver's licence could have been me. It was no problem renewing it and his health card. I got a job at a restaurant here in Rothesay. I couldn't give references, but they took me on a trial basis and saw I could cook. I stayed there for a couple of years. When the Gastropub opened they hired me, and I've been the chef of this restaurant since then."

"So what happened to make you run away from Halifax?"

Seamus hesitated for several seconds. "Serge Dimanche paid me to get out of town, and said he would kill me if I came back. He knew that I would testify against him at his trial. I'd managed his Halifax restaurant for several years, and I'd seen too many shady activities for me to want to stay there, so I quit. Then the police sniffed out his liquor fraud, and I was subpoenaed to testify. Serge gave me money for me to leave town which was enough to make a down payment on a house, so I settled back here. I haven't set foot in Nova Scotia since I left five years ago."

"You said that Serge Dimanche engaged in liquor law violations, what did he do exactly?"

"He buys contraband liquor and puts it into bottles of rye and scotch with well-known labels on them, selling them as the real thing. He also understates his sales to avoid taxes. Those are some of the things that I was aware of when I worked there, but I'm sure there are more. I'd put nothing past him."

"How has he succeeded in building a restaurant empire, and not being caught for so long?"

"I'm not sure. He's obviously been able to manipulate the authorities. But there's something strange about him. I suspect he's not what he pretends to be–a Frenchman who learned cooking in his grandmother's kitchen. I think he has a past that he's very careful not to reveal."

"Any guesses as to what that might be?"

Dooley looked away. "I haven't a clue," he said, but without much conviction. "So what do you do now? Turn me in to the police? I've told you what I know."

"You should consider voluntarily surrendering. The passage of time should help mitigate the punishment that you might face. And you wouldn't have to hide your identity any longer. With your testimony, Dimanche would probably be put behind bars."

"I'll think it over. Give me a few days to decide. And don't tell Dimanche or anyone else in Halifax about me in the meantime."

Dooley's cell phone rang. He got up and stepped away so that Hamish wouldn't hear the conversation. After a few minutes, he returned. "It was my daughter. She wanted to alert me that a detective had come around to talk to the super about her and her father. I told her you were here now, that you'd found me. She advises me to go to the police voluntarily."

13

Sean scratched his head. He was going over the route maps that AFS had given him. The head office had confirmed that most of the deliveries occurred on a Friday or a Monday. Fortunately, they had a record of the stops that were made on each of the days when some of the food was reported missing.

Each route, which was emailed in advance to the driver, listed the hotels and restaurants in the order of delivery. The route typically involved crossing the Macdonald Bridge from Dartmouth to Halifax, and going south-east along the waterfront, stopping first at Casino Nova Scotia and the Hotel Halifax, then making deliveries to restaurants on Upper and Lower Water Street. Finally, the delivery truck turned up South Street and wound its way back to the bridge, servicing several hotels and restaurants along the way.

Sean checked off the restaurants that had reported not receiving their full orders. These only began on Lower Water Street, after several earlier stops had been made. One of the earlier stops in each case was the BistroDimanche.

*****

On Friday, Sean pulled up to the warehouse in Dartmouth in his Subaru, parked, and went in search of Arturo. He had called him first to tell him of his plan.

Arturo was next to the refrigerated box truck parked at the loading dock, speaking to the delivery driver. "That's the last of the boxes. We've put them in the back of the truck, last-in, first-out, so you don't have to search through them each time. You're good to go."

Sean waved to Arturo, who gave the thumbs-up sign. Sean got back into his car, and, when the delivery truck pulled away from the warehouse, he followed it after a minute or so. Staying well back, he tailed it over the Macdonald Bridge. On the other side, Sean kept it in sight as the truck took the first exit and wound its way around to Barrington Street. When the driver pulled into the delivery entrance of the Casino Nova Scotia and backed up to its loading dock, Sean parked on the street in front. Cautiously, he walked around the building to the back. He could see that the driver had opened the rear door and had removed two boxes from the truck, laying them on the concrete floor of the delivery bay, before closing the cargo door. He scanned them and got the casino employee to initial a sheet on his clipboard. The driver then got in the truck and drove off.

Sean had been sent by email the list of delivery destinations, so he knew where the driver would go next. He parked near the Hotel Halifax, and was able to witness a similar procedure there, which took five minutes. The third delivery was scheduled for BistroDimanche. The truck pulled into an alley behind the restaurant, while Sean parked on a road leading from Upper Water Street to Hollis Street. There was no loading dock at the back of the restaurant. Instead, the driver pushed a button beside the door and waited for someone to let him in. After ten minutes he had not reemerged, so Sean went around to the front and looked through the window. The driver was sitting at the bar, with a glass in his hand, chatting with the bartender. Sean returned to the back alley, where the truck's rear door was now open. He could see a man, who appeared to be a waiter, rummaging through the boxes at the back of its cargo hold. He seemed to be searching for one in particular. When he found it, he slit the tape that covered its flaps and opened it, removing several of the packages. He pulled out a roll of tape and sealed the box once again before closing the truck door and going back into the restaurant with the packages.

Sean had surreptitiously taken some pictures with his cell phone. After another 10 minutes, the driver returned with the man Sean had seen taking things from the truck. The driver read the barcode on one of the boxes and handed it to the waiter. He closed the cargo door, then drove off to the next destination on the deliveries list, the Irish Alehouse, which was around the next corner.

Sean observed the delivery there, which only took five minutes and did not involve the driver going inside the restaurant. Sean decided that he had enough evidence, and, rather than continue tailing the truck, he returned to the AFS warehouse.

Arturo was taking delivery of some carrots, onions, and broccoli which he was getting an assistant to divide into bunches and to barcode. He waved to Sean: "Come into my office. You can tell me what you've got."

Sean waited until he was seated at Arturo's desk, with the door closed, before speaking. "Let me show you the pictures. You'll see right away what's been going on." He scrolled through his photo gallery and enlarged one of them. "This is a guy who came out of BistroDimanche. In the meantime, your driver was inside, having a drink at the bar. I have a picture of that, too."

"Oh my god, this isn't good! The guy from the restaurant's going through one of the other boxes, taking some stuff. I'm guessing it's the beef and salmon steaks. I'll call Shipping and tell them they have a rogue driver."

Sean shook his head. "Not so fast! Let's not show our hand quite yet. The guy from the restaurant obviously knew what to look for. After all, he only opened one box. So he must have been tipped off by someone at AFS. Besides, from the past deliveries that lost stuff we have to conclude that more than one driver was involved. In fact, the driver may not be the culprit, except that he left his truck unattended. Instead, we have to find the source of information on the contents of the boxes."

"Yeah, that could be what happened. And the info must have come from here or from head office, since shipping doesn't have a list of the things in the boxes, just the destination and the barcode of each box."

"It's clear that BistroDimanche is behind this, because the thefts have occurred with different drivers. Someone at the restaurant offers them a free drink. I'll bet it's known among the drivers that they can expect one when they stop there on a Friday. Maybe it's a TGIF type of thing, after a busy week–Thank God It's Friday."

"You're right, that's gotta be it. So how're you gonna find out who's the rat?"

"Let's wait and see who's missing some of their order and what it was. I'm going to talk to head office in the meantime to let them know what I found."

*****

Jeff Winding was behind his desk going over a list of orders when Sean arrived. He looked up. "We've had another delivery that was short. Four Points by Sheraton Hotel says they ordered a dozen steaks, but they weren't in the box we delivered to them today. I thought you were going to follow the delivery truck!"

"I did, and I found out where the food is getting stolen." He showed Winding the photos on his smartphone. "Now we've got to find out how BistroDimanche knew what box to look in. It's either someone here or in the warehouse who's sharing the information."

Winding pulled out a list of current employees. "There are only two people who handle the orders here at the head office, and in the warehouse there's three–Arturo, his assistant, and a clerk– who have access to them."

"Are any of them recent hires? The problems only started six months ago, right?"

"Let's see. Beth who takes down the phone orders has been here from day one. We can rule her out. There's Fred who goes through the emails, he's been here for two years. He's doing a business degree at night. I don't think he's our guy. Over in the warehouse there's more turnover. Except for Arturo, they are short-term hires. Let me get my assistant to dig out their applications for you."

"Here's what we could do to find out if BistroDimanche is getting tipped off by someone who works here or someone at the warehouse. Get your people to put together the list of orders for next Friday's deliveries, which they will transmit to the warehouse as usual. Then you personally phone Arturo to tell him that there's been a last minute change to one of the orders: it needs to include a dozen more steaks. You arrange with the restaurant to notify you whether those steaks show up with their order when it's delivered."

"OK, that makes sense. I'll set it up so that the additional steaks go on the order of a restaurant owner I know well. There'll be no problem getting the steaks back if they do get delivered to him, though it seems more likely that they will be stolen."

14

Sean filled Hamish in on the investigation of the missing food for AFS. "BistroDimanche is not just sabotaging your friend Des's restaurant, they're also stealing some of the food they serve from AFS. I'll bet they sell a lot of *steak-frites*, a staple of Parisian bistro cuisine. Since BistroDimanche gets some of their steaks for free, they must be making a whopping profit on them. Maybe this is a way for them to stay in business, despite their financial problems."

"So, when are you going to the police?"

"We're going to try to nab BistroDimanche in the act next Friday. I'll call Halifax Regional Police in the meantime. Who is it you used to know there?"

"I'll give Sam O'Leary a ring for you. He's in financial fraud. He can set up surveillance of the restaurant."

*****

Arturo made sure that all the boxes had been loaded before telling the driver that he was good to go. The order for the Westin Hotel had been augmented with a dozen steaks, which Fred Winding had told Arturo was a last-minute addition to their order. Apparently one of the private rooms of the hotel had been rented for a special dinner in honour of a retiring executive, and steak was on the menu.

The truck made its way as usual across the Macdonald Bridge and after a few stops pulled into the alley behind Bistro-Dimanche. Joe Hannity, a thirty-year-old who had worked as a driver since he had turned twenty-one, wore a blue uniform that bulged in places as his sedentary job was taking its toll on his physique. He rang the bell of the restaurant, and the door was opened by one of the waiters, whom Joe recognized as someone who used to work at *Bord de l'eau*. "Howya doin Jimmy? How's your new job?"

"Pretty much the same as the old one, it just pays better!"

Joe slapped him on the back, and was invited into the restaurant as expected for a drink.

It was nearing lunchtime on a Friday morning, and there were already a few patrons at the bar. The bartender came over, a big smile on his face. "What would you like?"

Joe had been thinking of what to order all morning. Once before he had been served something made of sparkling wine and some purple liqueur, he thought it was maybe black currant. It was good, and it must be expensive, he thought. "I'll have the *kir royale*, or whatever it's called. You know the one I mean?"

The bartender nodded. He took a bottle labelled *Crème de Cassis* from a shelf behind the bar. He poured some of the liqueur into a wine glass, took out a bottle from the fridge behind the bar, and added some sparkling white wine to the glass. After giving it a stir with a swizzle stick, he put it on the bar in front of Joe. "Voilà!" he said.

Joe gave it a sip. "Delicious!" He didn't have anything else to say to the bartender, who went down to the other end of the bar to talk to a regular.

One of the other men sitting there wandered to the back of the dining room. A hallway led to the men's and women's washrooms, but he continued to the end of the hall and went through a door that opened outside. Looking out at the back of the truck, he saw Jimmy, the waiter who had let Joe into the restaurant, inside the truck, searching through boxes. Jimmy looked up, startled.

"I'm arresting you on suspicion of theft." He showed Jimmy his Halifax Regional Police badge. Jimmy did not respond, nor did he resist when the policeman clipped handcuffs on his wrists. "You're coming down to the station with me."

He pushed Jimmy back through the rear door of the restaurant and hailed the bartender. "You at the bar: I'm arresting your waiter on suspicion of theft of food from the truck." He walked Jimmy out the front door to a police van parked down the street.

Joe was taken aback. He quickly finished his drink and went out to look in his truck. Everything seemed in order, so he continued to the next stop on his route.

*****

Sean was feeling pleased with himself as he sat in the conference room waiting for Jeff Winding to return. He had been called away to take an urgent phone call. A woman who was Winding's assistant came in to offer Sean something to drink in the meantime. Beth was an attractive blond in her thirties with ringlets in her hair. Her round face sported an amused smile.

Sean noticed that she didn't wear a wedding ring. With a grin he said: "A martini would be nice."

She laughed, then added with a sparkle in her eyes: "Maybe later! On Fridays some of us in the office go round after work to the Horse and Feathers for a drink. If you're free, you could join us."

At that point Jeff returned with a worried expression on his face. "That was Arturo. He's mad at us for not telling him that the extra order of steaks was bogus. He says it proves that he was under suspicion, and he's threatening to quit."

"Does he have any idea whether his assistant or the temp working at the warehouse are in cahoots with BistroDimanche? How does he think that the restaurant was tipped off?"

"That's just it. He claims that BistroDimanche doesn't have a spy at the warehouse. According to him, they could have learned about the steak orders in some other way. Maybe our phones are tapped. Or they could have installed a surveillance camera or something."

"Hmm. That's possible, I guess. You need to have a good look through the warehouse for spyware and check whether someone has hacked into your phones."

"Another thing: apparently the waiter at BistroDimanche has been released by the police. The owner, Serge Dimanche, sent a lawyer to get him out. The lawyer claimed that Jimmy was innocent of any intention to rob the truck. He was in the truck to save Joe from having to unload the box meant for BistroDimanche. As the lawyer pointed out, Jimmy had not opened any of the other boxes before being apprehended. Besides, Jimmy had only been at BistroDimanche for a few weeks, so it didn't make sense to argue that BistroDimanche had used him in a scheme that had been in operation for at least six months. So our plan to catch someone from BistroDimanche in the act of opening a box with the extra steaks has failed. The policeman acted a little too quickly. They've decided not to charge the waiter, and the case against BistroDimanche has evaporated."

"Oh, great! Now that they've been tipped off, we'll never get the evidence that we need to convict them. At least BistroDimanche is unlikely to use the trick of a free drink for the driver to hijack your deliveries in the future. So we did what you asked us to do."

"Yes, you did. Send us the invoice. I just wish it had turned out better."

*****

Sean's euphoria had turned to melancholy so when he left AFS's headquarters at the end of the afternoon he decided he needed a pick-me-up. Looking around for a place to have a drink, he saw the Horse and Feathers at the corner so he went in and sat at the bar. He ordered a martini and was about to take a sip when Beth came in with some of her colleagues, who headed to a booth on the other side of the room. Beth came over to talk to Sean. "So it didn't turn out the way you planned. I heard this from Jeff. Oh well. Need a shoulder to cry on?" She looked at him with a small smile on her lips.

Sean felt the need to find solace in someone's arms, and Beth would do nicely. "Thanks, I'll take you up on that! Let me order you a drink. How about a martini?" After another one each, they left arm-in-arm for Beth's apartment, which was in a highrise a few short blocks away, with a view of Halifax Harbour.

They took the elevator up to the tenth floor. Beth giggled as she rummaged through her purse for her keys. "Don't think that I do this every Friday night!" When they got inside she turned to him and kissed him on the mouth. He ran his hands down her back, then up the front of her blouse.

"Hey, let's slow down a bit." They went out on her balcony and watched the sunset for a few minutes. It was a marvellous evening, with a bright blue sky that was gradually darkening to indigo. Sean put his arm around her shoulders, and pulled her to him. She gave in this time, and started to pull up his shirt. In a minute, they were tumbling onto her bed in a frenzy of desire. Afterward, Beth daintily slipped out of bed and put on her robe, then rooted through the fridge for something to eat. "How about Chinese takeout, Sean? I'll order some Szechuan dishes, if that's OK."

They had dinner on the darkening balcony, illuminated only by the light filtering out from the living room. Sean told her about the detective business, how he and Hamish had come to partner together. Beth told him she had worked at AFS since getting a secretarial degree. "Being a detective sounds like more fun! I'm getting bored with my job."

"If we generate some more business, we might be able to hire an extra detective. I'll talk to my partner about that."

Sean accepted her invitation to spend the night. Sleep was interrupted by love-making a few more times. At six Sean woke up tired but happy. He pulled on his clothes, kissed the cheek of the still sleeping Beth, and went back to the AFS parking lot to retrieve his car and drive back to Ashcroft.

15

When Sean got back to the Oaks, he told Hamish about the failed bust at BistroDimanche. "So we're back to square one, though at least we've solved part of the mystery of the disappearing steaks! The more I think of it, though, I wouldn't be surprised that they are somehow monitoring the orders that are shipped out of AFS's warehouse. I told Jeff Winding that we didn't have the expertise to locate BistroDimanche's surveillance equipment. He should hire another firm for that, and probably get them to put in cameras to monitor his staff as well."

Hamish said with a sardonic smile: "When you didn't show up last night I was worried that you'd been caught in a crossfire between the police and Serge Dimanche! By the way, was he at the restaurant at all?"

"No, he never showed up, but he sent a lawyer to free his waiter. We don't know what his role was in the scam, but I'll bet he knew about it. Proving it is another matter."

"Hopefully he will lay off my friend Des's restaurant, at least for now. He must realize that he's in the crosshairs of the legal system, and if he's not careful they're going to bring him down."

"What happens to the fraud case against Dimanche if Seamus Dooley turns himself in to the police? Is Dimanche likely to be tried again after all these years?"

"It would be up to the Public Prosecution Service to decide whether to bring the case once more, with the additional charge of suborning a witness. But given the time that has passed, I suspect they would want to have some more recent evidence of criminal activity as well. I'll bet the Halifax Regional Police will be closely monitoring the source of the food and drink served at BistroDimanche restaurants from now on."

Sean sighed. "I'll be glad to see the end of our involvement in this. I hope not to hear about Serge Dimanche ever again!"

"That will depend on Des, and whether he still feels targeted by BistroDimanche."

*****

Des called Hamish the next day. "I'm still being harassed by you-know-who. This morning someone turned my trash bins upside down and spilled garbage all along the sidewalk in front of my restaurant. I'm waiting for the electronics outfit to install surveillance cameras, so for the moment I have no way of proving who did it."

"What would you like me to do? I can't stake out the restaurant 24/7."

"How about following Dimanche and confronting him? Do you think that would do any good?"

"After our altercation at the UNICEF Gala, I can't see the point of confronting him again. So I'd say no. Let me see if we can find out more info about him, and whether Seamus Dooley has surrendered to the police."

16

Sean and Marjoree went out sailing on one of the Ashcroft Yacht Club's sailboats, a Beneteau First 23.5 sloop that members could borrow. It was a glorious morning on the water: bright sunshine, mild temperature and a steady breeze. They went out into Mahone Bay, navigating around the numerous small islands there.

"How about going over to Chester? We should be able to go and come back on a beam reach, given the wind direction. We could dock at the Chester Yacht Club, have lunch nearby, and sail back."

"Sounds good to me. I know the place well. My husband and I used to be members of CYC years ago."

They found dockage without any problem, then walked to the Rope Loft for lunch, which was not too crowded despite it being noon on a weekday. As they were being seated in a rustic dining room, a large man with a deep tan waved to a waiter and proceeded to chew him out. "Where is my shrimp cocktail? It must have been made in advance, and it's served cold! So why have I been waiting for 20 minutes?!"

He was sitting at a booth, with an attractive woman elegantly dressed in a BCBG suit who looked to be in her 50s seated across from him. She said in French, "Serge, leave him alone; it's not his fault."

The waiter apologised profusely. " I think the cook wanted to add some fresh lime slices. That's the reason for the delay."

Sean nudged Marjoree. "I'll bet that's Serge Dimanche. I think I recognize him from his photos."

"Yes, that's him all right. I know his wife quite well. They joined the yacht club here when we were members. I think they still have a big Dufour sailboat. I should go over and say hello."

"Don't mention my name or what I do."

Marjoree approached their table and addressed the woman. "Hi Janine, do you remember me? Marjoree Price. My husband and I were members of the yacht club a long time ago."

"Marjoree, of course! It's good to see you. What brings you to Chester?"

"I'm just here for the day. We sailed over from Ashcroft." She nodded in Sean's direction.

"Why don't the two of you join us for lunch then? We haven't started eating yet, as you may have heard when you came in." Janine looked wryly at Serge.

When Sean came over she introduced Sean by his first name only, as a sailor friend. "We both live in Ashcroft."

Serge Dimanche merely nodded in his direction. He turned around angrily, as if to summon the waiter again.

Janine was fiddling impatiently with her silverware. "Will you behave yourself, Serge?" She turned to Marjoree. "Tell me what has happened since we last saw you. I was saddened to hear of your husband John's death. Then I thought you went into a retirement home?"

"That's right. But it turned out that they were treating us like guinea pigs, trying out antioxidants and omega-3 supplements on us without our permission. In the end, the home burned down and those responsible went to jail. I bought a townhouse in Ashcroft-by-the-Sea. What about you, Janine?"

"Well, we still live in Chester and are CYC members though our boat, *Finisterre*, is up for sale. Serge keeps talking about sailing her down to the Caribbean but other things get in the way. You'd think he could retire from the business and leave it to others to run the restaurants, but he still wants to keep his hand in it."

The waiter came with Serge's shrimp cocktail and a platter of deep fried calamari with aioli sauce, which Janine offered to share with Marjoree and Sean, who had only ordered a main course. The waiter had also brought a bottle of white wine. Serge tried the Sancerre, which he pronounced good. "I love the dry, flinty taste of this wine." He grudgingly agreed to let the waiter pour out four glasses.

After a glass of wine and his shrimp cocktail, Dimanche made an effort to be sociable. "So what do you do, Sean, when you're not sailing?"

Sean hesitated before responding. "Unfortunately, I mainly work at repairing my old house, which was built by my forebears in the 19th century. It's a large house, much too large for me, and the heating bills are enormous!" He was about to mention sharing it with Hamish Cameron, but bit his tongue.

Serge sympathized with Sean about the headaches of owning an old house. "That's why I had our house here in Chester custom built. At least I know where the skeletons are buried!" He laughed wickedly.

The waiter served their main courses, and conversation flagged. After eating their seafood and enjoying the wine, the four of them seemed more relaxed and in better humour.

"So you see," Janine said, turning to Serge, "we can all get along–at least over food and wine! That's one thing the French discovered centuries ago. It's too bad they and the Germans didn't have the same taste in food though–we might not have fought as many wars!" They all laughed.

The meal ended amicably enough, though the two men eyed each other warily as they said goodbye. Janine and Marjoree hugged and promised to stay in touch.

As they walked back to the yacht club, Marjoree said to Sean: "That was pleasant, wasn't it? Now you know what Serge is like. He's not really a bad sort." They got on their boat, started the little outboard engine mounted at the stern, and cast off.

The wind had died so they did not raise their sails but instead decided to motor back. They took a shortcut through a narrow channel between a peninsula of the mainland and an island, and Marjoree pointed out Dimanche's boat, which was docked at a long pier in front of a large house with white pillars. The mansion was situated on the mainland atop a hill, surrounded by a manicured lawn which led down to the water. Sean noticed a man on the terrace, looking at them through binoculars.

"That's some sailboat," Sean said, pointing at *Finisterre*. It measured more than 40 feet long, with a mast that towered over the deck. An inflatable dinghy was tied up at its stern, while a covered boat house next to the dock sheltered a classic wooden runabout in pristine condition. "Apparently Serge doesn't trust others to get too close to his boats, if that's him on the terrace." He waved at the man on shore, who did not wave back.

*****

"I bet you can't guess who I met in Chester!" Sean told Hamish when he returned to The Oaks. "Serge Dimanche and his wife, Janine! Marjoree knows her well, so we were invited to join them for lunch. Serge was pretty obnoxious to start with, but we ended up at least being civil to each other."

"I hope you didn't reveal who you were! Anyway, I have a hard time believing that you've made a new friend. You may end up helping to put him in jail!"

"If he learned that you've located his former employee, Sea- mus Dooley, who knows what he might do? We don't want Di- manche to have another opportunity to suppress his testimony."

"Let's wait and see what happens when Dooley surrenders to the police."

17

Janine

Janine was vaguely worried about her chance encounter with Marjoree and Sean. She had a feeling that Sean was not who he seemed. Her experience in French intelligence made her suspicious. He was too careful in his replies when Serge had asked him what he did. She did not want to have people poking into Serge's background. He had succeeded in making a new life for himself, putting his Stasi past behind him. It would be a shame to jeopardize everything now through carelessness. She would have to be cautious when talking to Marjoree, but she couldn't avoid her completely; that would just cause her to pry further. She decided to invite her over for tea.

In the meantime, she did some searching online for someone called Sean who lived in Ashcroft by the Sea. *Aha! He works for a detective agency, Cameron and Carroll. And hadn't Serge told her that the retired judge's name was Cameron? Maybe it wasn't a chance encounter after all. Sean might have been spying on us!*

Her husband's spat with Desmond was also starting to worry her. Was it just commercial rivalry, because they were both French restaurants and located close to each other, or was it something more? She had not spoken to Desmond since they were dating in Germany decades ago, but she had kept track of his restaurant's activities. She was the one who realized that Desmond had been behind the accusations five years ago that Serge served contraband liquor at BistroDimanche. She suspected that Desmond had encouraged their chef at the time, Seamus Dooley, to testify against her husband. She convinced Serge to bribe Dooley to clear out of town then as the best way to get rid of the problem. *I wonder if we should try to locate him, now that the fight with Desmond is heating up again. He can't have disappeared without a trace.* She searched the internet for the name Seamus Dooley, without success. *I'll get more details from Serge about his background. I'm sure I can track him down with a little more effort.*

18

It was Lobsterfest Night at the Ashcroft Yacht Club where Sean, Hamish, and Marjoree were having dinner. The dining room was full. For $35, members and their guests could have a hot or cold lobster and a serving of potato salad. Sean chose the hot entree, which came complete with a bib, a claw cracker, and a bowl of melted butter. "Delicious! I think this is the best lobster I've had in a long while."

Marjoree echoed his opinion. "I love my lobster salad, especially since it's served on a bed of lettuce with garlic mayonnaise. The lobster is just moist enough to be tender, and it's nice to have the shell removed and the meat already cut up rather than having to do it myself."

Hamish said with mock indignation: "Sorry to break into this food orgy, Marjoree, but would you please tell us what you know about Janine Dimanche and her husband?"

She reluctantly put down her fork. "Janine and I used to sit together at the club and chat when our husbands were crewing on the evenings of sailboat races. John and I were also occasionally invited out for a day sail on Serge's *Finisterre,* and we reciprocated by taking them out on our sailboat. Janine is a pleasant companion, and she speaks very good English. She treats Serge like a naughty child at times, but humours him. I asked her how they had met, but her comments about the past were always vague. She said they had lived in Paris, but not whether she had grown up there. She never told me what she did in France before coming to Canada."

"Why did they move to Canada–did she say?"

"Oh, the usual thing: better business opportunities, the chance of starting their own business, *et cetera*. Apparently they had made plans to open a bistro someplace when they first met, and Canada seemed to them to be a better place to do so than France, where they would have a lot more competition."

"Do you know what Serge did in France? Did he work in a restaurant? His bio gives no details about his prior experience."

"No, I've no idea. I had the impression, though, that Janine was the person who chose the menus and the decor of the restaurants here, at least initially, while he took care of the practical side of setting up and running the business. Of course, now the restaurants pretty much run themselves, since the menu never changes." She said impatiently: "Is that all; can I get back to my lobster?"

Sean glared at Hamish in mock anger. "You heartless brute! Your interrogation has kept her apart from her lobster!" He added with a smile: "Unfortunately it didn't yield much information either. Serge is very good at avoiding questions, but why does Janine do the same?"

The three of them returned to their lobster meals, but when they were done they were no further ahead in solving the mystery. Hamish turned to Marjoree. "Are you willing to do some more socializing with Janine? Maybe you can help us get to the bottom of this."

*****

"It's so nice to invite me over for tea, Janine," Marjoree said before biting into the scone that she had picked up from the silver tray in front of them. She had called Janine a few days before, suggesting that they meet for a drink to catch up, and had been invited to her house instead. Marjoree looked around at the sun-filled enclosed porch, with its view down to the water. "This is a lovely home. How long have you owned it?"

"We bought the building lot when our restaurants started making serious money. We wanted some place close enough to Bridgewater and Halifax, and on Mahone Bay where we could keep our boat. The lot came on the market just as we started looking, and we snapped it up, then built our dream home. Now I'm not sure we would be able to afford it."

"Have you always been a sailor? I imagine that growing up in France you had many opportunities when you were little." Marjoree spoke with a rising inflection, leaving it a question to be answered by her friend.

"No, not at all. I spent my childhood in a town on the out-skirts of Paris, far from the coast. I was introduced to sailing much later, by colleagues at work."

"Oh, what sort of work did you do?"

"Just office work." Janine looked around as if searching for another topic of conversation. "And yourself, how and where did you meet your husband, Marjoree?"

"We met at university in Halifax. John was studying busi-ness, I was in a humanities program. We got married soon after graduation. John started working for a big company based there, and I did this and that. At that time, a woman who worked was viewed as a sign that her husband couldn't make ends meet, so John didn't encourage me to do so. Instead, I joined various women's groups, did some charity work, and learned to play golf and sail. I know it must sound like a wasted life to you, since you were actively involved in getting BistroDimanche off the ground. How did you meet Serge, anyway?" She stared earnestly at Janine, making it difficult for her to sidestep the question.

"We crossed paths in Paris, meeting at a party given by someone both of us knew slightly. It was a chance encounter, but we immediately saw that we had things in common."

"Love at first sight, was it? And maybe love of food!" Marjoree chuckled. "Did Serge recount to you his grandmother's recipes?"

Janine laughed, but looked slightly embarrassed. "Not exactly. But he did say he was hoping to get into the restaurant business, and I was looking for a more challenging occupation than the office work I was doing. One thing led to another, and soon we were planning to start a restaurant in Canada. Serge had heard that there were more opportunities here than in France, and the idea of living in a new country with its wide-open spaces was attractive to both of us."

Serge came in from outside, wearing his gardening boots, which he removed and left by the door. He greeted Marjoree heartily. "What have you and Janine been nattering about? It sounds as though you are raking over old coals! That's *inutile*—we must all look ahead, not behind us. We've got to make the best of the present, not worry about the past! In any case, my life only really started when I met Janine." He looked slyly over to his wife, who reddened slightly but didn't say anything.

Marjoree couldn't resist saying, "But what about growing up in your grandmother's kitchen? Wasn't that a major milestone in your life?"

Serge coughed. "Of course! But I was only a boy then, not the man I was to become," he said without much conviction. "Anyway, I'm going to open a nice Rhone wine, made where I used to live. Would anyone else want some?"

The conversation drifted off to other topics–sailing and gardening, and how the warm wet weather had been good for his roses. Marjoree discreetly looked at the label on the wine bottle, which had a Cairanne appellation. After another half hour she thanked her hosts for the delightful afternoon and drove back to Ashcroft.

19

Seamus

Seamus walked absently around his living room, looking over his meagre possessions. The visit from Hamish Cameron had destroyed his confidence that he had eluded people in Halifax who wanted to track him down. He thought that he had left that part of his life behind, but it was coming back to haunt him. People who might want to find him included Serge Dimanche and the police, but also Desmond Stuart. He turned over in his mind the alternatives he had to choose from at the moment— none of them was very pleasant. All of them probably meant abandoning the house that he had bought with Dimanche's money. He could try to run away and assume a new identity, as he had done before. It was clear now that this hadn't worked, however. Or he could turn himself into the police and face the likelihood of going to jail. At least he could sign the house over to his daughter beforehand, who could sell it and keep some proceeds for him. Assuming that he could trust her not to keep them all for herself.

Doing nothing wouldn't cut it, because that fellow Cameron wasn't going to let him go back to life as usual. If only he had stopped Mary from posting that photo of the two of them at the Reversing Falls! You couldn't be too careful these days, what with search engines poring over the web to find the faintest trace of your past life. If he decided to run away, he would have to change his appearance and cut off all contact with his daughter. He didn't want to do that, though. It wasn't likely to work, anyway. So maybe he should turn himself in. Cameron didn't leave him much choice. If he didn't go voluntarily to the police, soon they would come looking for him with information provided by the former judge, and he would almost surely get a stiff prison sentence. At least if he turned himself in, he could hope to benefit from some clemency.

In either case, he needed to destroy some papers that he had brought back from Germany because they might incriminate him. Those had been good times, though! He and Des had a comfortable life then, making double what they should have earned by sharing the invoices that they used for billing their respective armies. Fortunately, military bureaucracies were all alike: hung up on protocols and hierarchies so that no one did any thinking. The troops just followed orders and assumed that everyone else did too. It just took someone with an independent streak to cheat the system and get away with it. Too bad that German reunification had to happen—otherwise he could still be there living the good life! If he left his souvenirs of Germany in the house, including details of the provisioning scheme with

Desmond, then the Canadian Forces would learn about it and cancel his pension. He couldn't risk that happening.

Seamus was about to go down to the basement to look through his papers when he heard something outside. It sounded like a car crunching the gravel in his driveway. He looked out the living room window and spotted a black SUV parked in front of the garage. A loud rapping at the door was accompanied by a call to open up. Seamus squared his shoulders and marched towards the door, wishing that he had some sort of weapon with which to confront his visitors.

20

"Mr. Cameron, this is Mary Carstairs. You left your card with the super in my building. I'm worried about my father, Seamus Dooley. He doesn't answer his phone. I called the restaurant, and he didn't turn up yesterday. They had to scramble to get a replacement. Have you heard from him since the two of you talked last week?"

"No, I haven't. I've been hoping to learn from the Halifax police that he has surrendered voluntarily. Let me call them to find out. Have you been to his house?"

"Not yet, I've been too busy. I'll go there now."

*****

Sam O'Leary answered Hamish's call at the fifth ring. "Seamus Dooley, eh? You mean the mystery witness who never showed up to testify in your court about five years ago? Nope, I haven't heard anything about him, he hasn't contacted us. What's the story, anyway, Judge?"

"It's a long story, and I can't give you all the details now. I located him in New Brunswick, and I thought I had convinced him to turn himself in voluntarily to the police there. If he does, I'm sure that the Kennebecasis Regional Police will contact you.

But it seems instead that he's disappeared a second time. His daughter's trying to locate him. I'll let you know if we find him."

*****

Mary Carstairs called back a few hours later. "I went to his house, but there's no sign of him. And his truck is gone." She muffled a sob. "I don't understand how he could leave without telling me! He had agreed to surrender to the police. We were going to sort through his stuff together first. I was waiting for his call."

"Did he take things with him, like his clothes and papers?"

"Not that I could see. I noticed that his cell phone was still on the kitchen counter."

"I don't want you to be alarmed, but I would suggest that you call the local police and hospitals in case he's had an accident."

*****

"Kennebecasis Regional Police Force. How can I help?" The female voice was brisk but sympathetic.

Mary blurted: "My father has gone missing. Can you tell me if there are any reports of accidents locally that he might be involved in? He drives a black Ford F-150. His name is Kevin Martin."

"Hold on a sec, I'll check." After a minute, the police receptionist returned. "There's a report from the attendant at a golf course on Golden Grove Road that a pickup went into nearby Dolan Lake. We've sent a tow truck and a diver there to pull it out."

Mary grabbed her keys and purse and ran to her car, an ageing Toyota Corolla. Rush hour traffic hadn't yet started, so she made good time going north. She had to keep herself from driving even faster. *I don't want to be stopped for speeding!* She keyed Dolan Lake into her GPS, which told her to turn off Highway 1 at Coldbrook and take Golden Grove. The two-lane road was serpentine, so she had to slow down. *Only five kilometres more.*

The road passed several other lakes. Each time she took her foot off the accelerator, thinking that she had arrived. As she approached Dolan Lake, she slowed to 40 kph and looked for signs of activity. After rounding the north shore of the lake, at a spot where another road merged with Golden Grove she spotted a police cruiser beside the road, and pulled in beside it.

A young policeman in uniform was directing the tow truck driver, who was backing down a slope in a clearing that led to the lake. "Don't go too far, it looks soft there." There were tire marks already visible in the damp earth. Looking in the direction they were taking, Mary spotted the black roof of a vehicle that was just beneath the surface of the lake.

A woman wearing a wetsuit, flippers, and a mask was waiting along the shore. The tow truck stopped. The driver shouted to her: "That's as far as I want to go. Take the towing cable out to the pickup truck, and attach it to its bumper."

The policeman noticed Mary for the first time. "Lady, you can't park there. This is an accident scene." He motioned for her to get back into her car.

"I think it might be my father! He's been missing for several days. Can I at least see if that's his truck!" She was obviously distraught. *I just hope there's no one in there!*

"OK, OK, just stay out of the way. When we pull the truck out, you can tell us if it belongs to him."

The diver waded out into the lake, holding the cable with both hands and unspooling it from the winch on the tow truck. When she reached the pickup, she dove under water and attached the hook of the cable to its rear bumper. Wading back to shore, she gave the thumbs up to the tow truck operator.

The winch took up the slack on the cable. When it was taut, the grinding noise of the winch increased in volume but the cable would not advance further. He motioned the diver over: "Would you check to make sure that there's no tree trunk or rock preventing the wreck from moving?"

Wading out again, she put on her goggles when she got to the truck. She submerged and circled it under water. Resurfacing, she called: "There's nothing in the way. It must be the weight of water in the bed."

"OK, I'll use my engine to tow her out." The driver put his truck into its lowest gear, and started forward without gunning the motor. At first there was no progress. Then, the vehicle in the water broke free of the mud and was slowly pulled onto the shore, the tow truck stopping just before reaching the road.

The policeman walked around to the driver's side and carefully looked through the window, which was in the closed position. The cab was full of water, but he could make out a body slumped in the driver's seat. He motioned to the others. "OK, everybody out. We're going to need to investigate the cause of death. The wreck stays here."

Mary started sobbing. "It looks like my father's truck, all right. Can't I just see if it's him?"

"No way. A detective needs to examine the scene first. I'd like you to wait at the Rothesay police station until that's done. We can't have footprints and fingerprints everywhere."

*****

Mary had been waiting at the police station for two hours before the policeman who had told her to stay there returned from the accident scene. He introduced himself as Constable Jeremy Lepreau. "Ms. Carstairs, would you mind coming with me to see if you can identify the body before we take it to the morgue? You can follow me in your car."

The pickup truck's doors had been opened and the water drained out. The body was on a stretcher, with a tarp over it. Lepreau raised the tarp at one end, displaying the head. "Is that your father?"

Mary felt faint, and desperately tried not to fall to the ground. "Yes, it's him!" She began sobbing. "What could have happened? I have no idea why he would have come down this road!"

"The coroner still has to examine the body, but at this point it looks like an accident. He probably drove down McGill Road in the dark, and didn't realize that it met Golden Grove at a T-junction. He must have gone right through it, into the lake. An attendant at the golf course saw the truck this morning and called us to report the accident. It's not clear exactly when it occurred–sometime during the night. The coroner will try to determine the time and cause of death."

*****

Mary called Hamish to let him know. "I can't understand why he would be out driving in the middle of the night. If it had been daylight he would surely have stopped at the intersection, but anyway there was no reason he should have been on the road at all. We'd decided that I would come to his house to sort out his things before he surrendered to the police."

"Did he have things stored somewhere else? Perhaps a friend he was going to see? Or had he changed his mind, and was running away?"

"No, he had some friends in town but not out in the countryside. And I'm sure he would have told me if he had a change of heart."

"Did he ever reveal to you exactly why he fled Halifax five years ago? He must have given some explanation for taking someone else's name."

"He told me he was in danger of being killed or arrested. I presumed that he had been threatened by Serge Dimanche, his employer whom he was supposed to testify against. Since he did not testify, shouldn't he have been safe from Dimanche? I never knew exactly what was going on."

"It's strange that his accident happened so soon after I located him, especially since you say he had no particular reason to be on that road."

"Would you look into his death for me? I haven't told the police his true identity, and I don't want to explain the circumstances of his leaving Halifax to avoid testifying at the trial. I can't pay you much, but I'd like to know what happened."

"I can do that for you. I'll try to get the police to open up to me, but I'll have to reveal to them some of the background, including his real name and why I came looking for him. Are you OK with that?"

"I guess so. There's nothing they can do to him now."

Marjoree picked up the office phone. "Cameron and Carroll, Investigators. How may I help you?"

The voice at the other end of the phone hesitated. "This is Beth Phillips from AFS Logistics. May I speak to Sean Carroll, please?"

"Just a moment." Marjoree put her on hold. "Sean, do you know someone called Beth Phillips? She's calling from AFS. Do you want to take the call?"

Sean's face turned pink. "I guess so, sure. Uh, would you mind fetching the file on the AFS case? I think it may be in the car."

"OK, here, take the phone." Marjoree went out by the side door.

Sean said hesitantly, "Beth? How are you?"

"I'm fine, Sean. I'm so excited! I think I solved the mystery of how the waiter at BistroDimanche knew what box contained the high value food items on the delivery truck. You remember how I said that the detective business sounded a whole lot more interesting than the work that I was doing? Anyway, I decided to try it out in practice! I had an idea how someone could find out without having a spy at AFS."

"That sounds intriguing. Tell me more."

"Well, you know that I enter the phone orders into our database so that the warehouse can collect the products and put them in a box for shipping to deliver? In principle, only HQ and warehouse have access to that database. But the barcode readers do too! Since we need the barcode readers to update inventory in real time, they must communicate with the database via the internet. In practice, it means that they have a built-in cell phone that is programmed with the login procedure and pass-word needed to get into it. If someone has our barcode reader and is sufficiently knowledgeable about the technology, she can install a more powerful app that can read as well as write into our database."

"That makes sense. So do you have proof that that's what happened?"

"Not proof, but a good indication. I checked with shipping to discover if all the readers are accounted for. It turns out that one is missing! We had a delivery truck driver who just worked for us for two months. When he quit, he kept the barcode reader. We tried to get it back, but we couldn't get in touch with him–he seemed to have disappeared. In the end, we just docked his final wage payment to make up for it."

"Bravo! It looks as though you'd make a good detective. We should discuss this some more, maybe at your place?"

Marjoree came back inside, shrugging her shoulders as if to say that she couldn't find the file Sean wanted. He said into the phone: "This isn't the best time now, though. I'll be back in touch with you soon. Goodbye." Turning to Marjoree, he said, "I guess you couldn't find it. I'll look for it myself, then get back to AFS on the issue that they asked me about. Thanks for looking."

"Sure. So who is this Beth person anyway? I haven't heard you mention her before."

"Just a staff assistant at AFS. She enters the order information into their inventory system. She just discovered how some outsider tapped into their database."

"I thought we had done with AFS. After all, I sent them an invoice."

Sean looked embarrassed. "Well, maybe not."

22

Hamish drove to Rothesay via the Trans-Canada Highway and New Brunswick Route 1. He had called the Kennebecasis Regional Police first, and spoken to Constable Lepreau, saying that he wanted to visit the station to talk to him about the death of Kevin Martin.

It was a rainy morning when Hamish set off, taking Routes 103 and 102 to Truro, and then the Trans-Canada highway. The scenery was of little interest, and Hamish had taken it so many times he didn't even bother to look at the view. The Cobequid Pass section of the Trans-Canada no longer charged tolls for cars with Nova Scotia plates, so he cruised through the toll plaza without stopping. NB-1 was easy driving on the four-line divided highway that led through largely wooded land with scattered villages along the way.

In about five hours he was in Rothesay. He drove up to the low-rise police building on Millennium Drive, parked, and asked for Lepreau at the reception desk.

After a few minutes, a pleasant-faced young man of medium height, fit looking, thin and muscular, came out to greet Hamish. "Come on back, we can chat in one of the interview rooms without being disturbed. But first, what's your interest in Mr. Martin's death?"

"It's a long story. Can we sit down first? It's going to take some time to explain. But the short answer is that I've been hired by Mary Carstairs to find out what I can about her father's death."

They went along a corridor, at the end of which Lepreau opened a door that led to a room, sparsely furnished with just a plain rectangular wood table and three straight-backed chairs. They sat on opposite sides.

"So, what's the long story about your interest in Kevin Martin?"

Hamish cleared his throat. "The truth is, his real name is Seamus Dooley. He was wanted by the police, because he skipped out before he could testify at a trial five years ago of his former employer at a restaurant in Halifax. Apparently, the employer bribed him to do so. Dooley took a new identity and settled back in New Brunswick, near to where he grew up. I came looking for him because I'm investigating that restaurant owner once again."

"So how did you happen to come across Seamus Dooley's name? The trial, as you say, was a long time ago."

"I was the trial judge then, later retired, and I'm now part of a detective agency."

"Wow, that's some resume!" Lepreau laughed. "I guess I can share the police findings with you. But what you said has put them in a new light, and I think we're going to have to investigate further."

"How so?"

"Examination of the vehicle, a pick-up truck, showed no evidence of foul play, and the coroner's post-mortem found no traces of drugs in his bloodstream. There was a small amount of alcohol, but not enough to impair his driving. The Coroner concluded that the victim drowned after the truck crashed in the water. A contusion on his forehead was consistent with his being knocked unconscious by the collision, though he was wearing a seatbelt and the airbag had deployed. So the death was ruled accidental, probably caused by the inattention of the driver. However, one detail doesn't quite fit. Tire marks that match those of his truck were found beside the road near to the T-junction, and those of a second vehicle that was parked behind it. It seems that Dooley's truck stopped there before it made the plunge into the water."

"Yes, that wouldn't be consistent with the story of driver error. I think you need to find out who was in that second vehicle. Do you have photos of the tire prints?"

"Now that you've explained that the victim was hiding from the police and perhaps his former boss, that loose end takes on more significance. Yes, we have the tire prints, but the detective investigating this has moved onto another case, so he's not going to be able to look into it further."

"Mind if I poke around? "

Lepreau seemed happy to hear that. "I can't stop you. Just make it clear to anyone you talk to that you're not from the police. And let me know what you find."

*****

Seamus Dooley's house was a bungalow located in a wooded development with good sized lots, a few kilometres from the

Gastropub where he worked. Hamish was sceptical that any of the neighbours would have noticed a car stopping at Dooley's house, but he tried the closest neighbour. The doorbell rang loudly but no one came to the door. The nearest house on the other side was several hundred metres away, so Hamish gave up.

It was time for lunch. He decided to visit the restaurant where he had found Dooley. On his way to an empty table, he stopped by the bar.

The bartender came over and glared at Hamish. "You again! What do you want this time? A couple of days after you came in here he died!"

"Did anybody come looking for him after I did? Any suspicious characters?"

"Now that you mention it, a guy came in and asked to talk to the chef. Not from around here. It was his day off. The guy asked where Martin lived, and I gave him his address. Maybe I shouldn't have."

"What did he look like?"

"He was a fat guy, probably at least 60. He didn't say what he wanted with Martin. I looked outside when he left and saw that there was someone else in the car, but I couldn't make out whether it was a man or a woman. They were driving a black SUV with Nova Scotia plates."

"I don't suppose you noticed the car's make or plate number?"

"Nah, no such luck."

*****

After a burger and fries Hamish drove back to Dooley's house. Mary had told him that there was a key under the mat at the side door. He let himself into the kitchen. There were dirty dishes in the sink, and food in the fridge. *It doesn't look as though he was preparing to leave*, he thought.

There were two bedrooms on the main level. The bed in one of them had been slept in and not made up again. Its closet was full of men's clothes, but some of them were on the floor, and the bedside tables had their drawers pulled out and emptied on the floor. An office likewise seemed to have been searched. Hamish went down to the basement. Nothing there seemed out of place, there was a tool bench and some boxes with books and old clothes. He leafed through them, without noticing anything of interest. There were some books on European history and some mystery stories, plus old high school yearbooks.

Hamish took a few photos, got into his car, and drove back to Highway 1.

23

Hamish stopped by the Rothesay police station on his way back to Ashcroft. Lepreau was out, so he left him a note. "Two men were asking for the victim three days ago at the restaurant where he worked. Their car had Nova Scotia plates. I'll call you if I find out anything more."

*****

"The puzzle," Hamish said to Sean back at home, "is how Dimanche found out about Dooley–if it was indeed Dimanche and his henchman who asked for him at the restaurant. Until I visited Mary Carstairs' apartment building, I had no idea where I might find him. I didn't call anybody, so there's no way they could have learned about his location except by following me. But the two guys showed up two days later."

"You're ignoring at least three other possibilities. They could have learned where you went by planting a satellite tracking device on your car. They could have hacked into your phone, and received continuous data on your location through the phone's GPS. Or Desmond Stuart could have let it slip, and the information somehow got back to Dimanche. Tell you what,

I'll look over your car, and install a cybersecurity app on your phone to search for malware."

Hamish handed over his Samsung smartphone to Sean, who asked him for the password to unlock the screen.

"I don't use it, and I haven't bothered with the fingerprint scan either."

"Uh-oh. You really should. You're making it too easy for someone to get at your files, your emails, and probably your bank accounts and credit card numbers. You need to clear the phone's memory and go back to the factory settings. Then you can be sure that if malware was installed, it isn't there any more."

"But how could someone put a virus on my phone? I keep it on me at all times when I'm out of the house."

"You might have opened an attachment or followed a link that was bogus. There are also devices that can get into your phone using WiFi or Bluetooth, if it's not password protected. They just need to be in range. You may have been hacked when you went to Dimanche's Halifax restaurant."

"Oh no! Let's fix my phone right now. I don't feel safe anymore."

"I'll reset the phone to its status when you got it, getting rid of all new apps and extensions. Then you'd better enable the screen lock." After doing this, Sean did a quick search of the car to make sure it was not also bugged. "Seems OK," he told Hamish.

"It seems that I underestimated my opponent," Hamish said. "He's obviously using very sophisticated means to get what he wants. I've got to find out more about Dimanche's background."

24

Hamish tried to explain himself in his rudimentary French. *"Je voudrais parler à l'inspecteur Faucher, s'il vous plaît."*

"Je suis désolé. Il n'y a personne de ce nom à notre service."

Hamish had called the number he had for his friend, but it was many years old. He concluded from the operator's answer that Faucher had probably moved to a different job and changed his number. *"Est-ce que vous pouvez trouver son numéro? C'est Henri Faucher. Il est un vieil ami à moi."* He hoped that the woman at the other end of the call would take pity on him for his helplessness and consult a directory to find his friend's current phone number.

"Un instant, s'il vous plaît." After a minute, she was back on the phone. *"Il y a un certain Henri Faucher qui travaille pour la DGSI, la Direction Générale de la Sécurité Intérieure. Je vous passe son secrétariat."* She transferred his call to another agency, one which was concerned with French domestic security. The DGSI was the French equivalent of Britain's MI5.

Hamish explained to the person he was now connected to that he wanted to speak to an old friend, Henri Faucher, and he left a number for Faucher to call him back. Not expecting this to produce any result, he was pleasantly surprised to get a call half an hour later and hear the voice of his friend.

"*Salut, Hamish, quel plaisir de reprendre contact avec toi!*"

"A pleasure for me too to talk to you again, Henri. It's been a long time–too long!" Hamish had met Henri at a conference on legal issues that Hamish had attended with Izzie half a dozen years before. Henri was a lawyer working for the French security services, in particular involved in counter-terrorism and financial fraud.

"You probably don't know it, but I've retired from my judgeship and am now involved with a detective agency. I'm doing some investigating of a fellow who emigrated from France to Canada some time ago, in the 1990s, Serge Dimanche. Do you know anything about him? He apparently lived in Cairanne at some point. He claims to have spent his childhood in Provence, and learned how to cook there. He runs a chain of French restaurants here in Nova Scotia."

"Serge Dimanche, Serge Dimanche, that name rings a bell. I'll have a look to see if we have a *fiche*–how do you say it, a file?–on him. I'll let you know. Is Izzie well? Still teaching law at one of your universities?"

They exchanged small talk and Henri ended the call by promising to get back to Hamish with any information he was able to find.

*****

The next day Hamish received another call from Paris from Henri Faucher. "Hamish, I was right in thinking that the name Serge Dimanche was familiar. He moved to France in the early

1990s from Germany, and bought a vineyard in Cairanne. We don't know his exact origins, but suspect that he came from East Germany. After German reunification in 1990 and the break-up of the Soviet Union the year after, a lot of people took advantage of the newly opened border to leave the east to get jobs in the western part of the country. Those who were lucky enough to have savings in the East German currency, or Ostmark, were suddenly much richer, since their worthless currency was converted at a one-to-one rate into Deutsche Marks. I suspect that Dimanche was one of those, which is why he could afford to buy the vineyard. Unfortunately, a lot of the East German files were lost or destroyed, so we don't know for sure where he actually lived before becoming a resident of France. In 1992, he married a French woman, Janine Desprès, and they lived in Paris together. Subsequently, they left France for Canada."

"How did you happen to have a file on him, Henri? Was he viewed as a security risk?"

"When he arrived in France he had a German identity card but no other documentation. At that point in time, we still kept track of foreigners who could have been planted as Cold War spies–not that we had any proof that Dimanche fitted that description. Of course, that was a long time ago."

"I have another question. What do you know about Serge Dimanche's wife, Janine? She's a puzzle to us."

"Ah, *la belle Janine*. We don't have a file on her, but it's not because we were not interested in her. *Au contraire*. But I can't say anything more about her. I hope you will understand. I'm sorry, I have to go now to attend a meeting."

"Many thanks, Henri. Any chance you could come and see us here in Canada? Izzie and I would love to see you again!"

"That would be very nice. I will keep that in mind, and if the opportunity arises, I'll certainly get in touch with you."

25

The promised tropical storm was finally about to hit Nova Scotia, after moving up the east coast of the United States and being downgraded from hurricane status. The wind was picking up, and was starting to roar through the trees and rattle loose boards at The Oaks. Sean had closed most of the shutters, and moved patio furniture into a shed next to the house. "Hamish, you need to park your car in the barn, otherwise it may get hit by falling branches. I hope we aren't going to get as much rain as forecast. They say as much as 50 centimetres could fall, but they often overestimate just to make sure people take the storm seriously. If we get that much then the basement will surely flood."

After battening things down as much as possible, they retreated into the office to review what they knew about Serge Dimanche.

"Sean, we need to get tire prints of his car. As it stands, he seems to be a prime candidate for Dooley's murderer. What about going out to his house at night, and taking pictures of the treads using a flash?"

"That's not going to give you more than a small fraction of each tire's treads. What we should do is get him to drive through mud that's not too soft, and then take pictures of that. We don't know whether he even keeps a car outside, rather than in a garage."

"And how do we get him to drive through mud?"

Sean pondered that for a moment. "With all this rain we might be able to get a good set of prints if we could time it right. But if we don't, then the rain might just wash them away before we get a chance to take photos! Maybe we go back to Plan A. Let's try to scope out his place before the storm comes with full force, and decide how to proceed. OK with you?"

"Let's do it."

*****

They took Hamish's Prius. They wound along the shoreline in the face of rising wind. Wind gusts threatened to blow them dangerously close to the water. Hamish slowed down. After half an hour they came to Chester. After passing through the centre of town, they continued on a gravel road with a Dead End sign on it that was lined with houses, most of which built on the left side of the road so that they had waterfront. At its end was the Dimanche estate. Water was starting to puddle on the road. They saw a light green Fiat 600 parked near the front door, on a circular driveway that led back to the road. A three-car garage, with white siding like the rest of the house, was attached to it. Its doors were shut, so it was impossible to tell what vehicles might be inside. There was no one in front of the house, but large fir trees prevented them from seeing into the backyard.

There was no place to park near the house without going into the driveway. Hamish said: "We're going to look conspicuous if we stay here for more than a minute. We'll have to turn around."

He made a U-turn out of the cul-de-sac and drove the Prius back into town, no wiser than when they started.

"Maybe we can lure Serge to his restaurant, and get a look at his tires there," Sean suggested. "He must go in occasionally."

"When I talked to his combination chef and manager in Halifax, the fellow said that Dimanche wanted any requests to go through the head office in Bridgewater. I'll bet that's a more likely place to find him. Let's swing by there to have a look."

On the outskirts of Chester, Hamish took the Fishermen's Memorial Highway toward Bridgewater, which they reached thirty minutes later. "I looked up the address, it's on the right bank of the LaHave River. I'll cross the river and park nearby, where we can have a look without raising suspicions."

The wind was whipping up whitecaps on the river as they crossed the bridge. The BistroDimanche headquarters was in a modest two-story building with wood siding painted red. A black BMW SUV was parked in a concrete-surfaced driveway next to it. They went by, made a U-turn, and parked on the street a hundred metres away, affording them a clear view of the front of the building.

"I think you're in luck, Hamish. I doubt if any of the staff could afford that car. Dimanche must own it. But how are we going to get his tire prints without showing ourselves? He's met both of us and would probably recognize us if we approach the building in daylight."

"It looks as though there's enough dirt in the driveway for a car tire to leave a good impression if he backs out. The rain's not so heavy that it will obliterate the tread marks right away. So we'll wait until Dimanche leaves, and zip over there to take pictures. It's 5 o'clock now, and I'll bet it's about closing time."

Fifteen minutes later, a middle-aged lady with her grey hair in a severe bun exited the front door and pulled a hood over her head. She quickly got into an old Nissan Sentra parked on the street and drove away. A few minutes later, a man in his twenties dressed in an anorak and wearing horn-rimmed glasses emerged. He let a rain-coated Dimanche out, and then locked the door. Dimanche got into his car, while the other man walked down King Street, passing Hamish's Prius with his head down without looking their way.

After Dimanche had backed out his BMW and driven away in a direction opposite to that where the Prius was parked, Hamish quickly got out. He took several photos of the driveway between the curb and where the BMW had been parked using his cell phone. Given the stormy weather there were no pedestrians so he did not attract attention. When he got back to the car, he was smiling broadly. "Let's see what the police make of these prints!"

*****

The wind had picked up further, but they got back to The Oaks without mishap and parked the car in the barn next to the house. Hamish quickly emailed photos of the tire prints to Jeremy Lepreau in Rothesay while the network was still up. He attached a note. "These were taken from a BMW SUV. Please let me know if they match the prints found near to the place Seamus Dooley drowned." He copied the email to Sam O'Leary.

As the storm intensified, the power went out and cell phone coverage was intermittent. It wasn't until the following day that Hamish received Lepreau's answer. "Your prints are of Continental tires that match those at the drowning scene. The tread pattern is identical to those we found on the side of the road. Unfortunately, both sets of tires have little wear on them, however, so it's not possible to be sure that the treads are from the same car. We intend to investigate further. My boss has decided to reopen the case on the assumption that Dooley's death was not an accident."

26

The wind had abated and the rain mostly passed over. Sean spent most of the morning assessing the damage and picking up tree limbs. A large branch had broken off one of the oaks. "I'll have to get an arborist to come in to clean up the yard and trim the trees. The basement is damp but fortunately doesn't need to be pumped out. I'll just run the dehumidifier."

"So it could have been a lot worse! At least the power is back up. A lot of the province isn't so lucky."

"That's true. Anything new in the Dimanche case?"

"The Kennebecasis police are putting together a circumstantial case against Serge Dimanche with the help of the Halifax Regional Police, which is also involved since Seamus Dooley was their witness. His disappearance meant that Dimanche got off scot free. What they don't have is a convincing motive. Why was Dooley so dangerous for Dimanche that he felt it necessary to kill him, after all these years? It's true that Dimanche might have faced a prison term if Dooley had testified. But the maximum penalty for witness tampering under the Criminal Code is five years, and Dimanche's sentence might well have been less."

"You don't actually know that it was Dimanche who was in the car that visited Dooley's restaurant, do you? And who was the other guy?"

"I'm guessing that it's the chef of the Halifax restaurant. He would fit the description, anyway, and that's the flagship Bistro-Dimanche so you'd expect his closest associates to work there. But you're right, we just don't know. We need to try to find out his whereabouts on the night when Dooley went off the road, and those of Dimanche."

"How do we do that?"

"Why don't you go down to the restaurant on Water Street at dinner time, and talk to the bartender or one of the waiters? I'd do it except that they know me there. You didn't go into the restaurant when you were tailing the delivery truck, did you? If not, you should be able to get someone to talk."

"OK, I can do that. I know someone I owe a dinner to. It will look less suspicious if there are two of us."

*****

Sean had arranged for Beth to meet him at the BistroDimanche restaurant on Upper Water Street. She took the ferry over from Dartmouth, then walked a few blocks to the restaurant. Sean was sitting at a table, looking towards the door. He waved when he saw Beth, and she joined him. The restaurant was mostly empty at six o'clock on a Tuesday evening, as the city was still reeling from the tropical storm.

Beth gave him a little kiss on his cheek after sitting down. "This is nice, Sean. What's the occasion?"

Sean looked slightly embarrassed. "I just wanted to see you, and I also promised a friend to try to track down his sunglasses so that's why I wanted to come here. It's nice to get out a bit after hunkering down at home while the storm raged. How did you make out?"

"Oh, no problem. But then my apartment building is pretty new and well constructed. And my car is in an underground parking garage which didn't flood."

A uniformed waiter, a slender man with a tattoo on his right arm, came over with two menus. He seemed to be in his early twenties, and Sean suspected that he was still in university but making some money by working part time in the evening. "Tonight, we have all our regular dishes, as listed in the menu and on the chalkboard. Can I get you something to drink while you decide? A glass of wine, perhaps, or mineral water?"

"I'll have a glass of white wine," Sean replied. "But tell me, do you work here every night? A friend of mine lost his sunglasses, and I promised to find out if there was a pair that was left here Saturday night. My friend couldn't remember where he'd left them."

"I wasn't here then, because the restaurant was closed to the public for a special gala dinner that our boss, Serge Dimanche organized to raise funds for Ukraine humanitarian relief. So unless your friend attended, he must have left his sunglasses somewhere else. I can ask the bartender anyway, if you like."

"Oh, so Mr. Dimanche would have been here all evening?"

"Yes, apparently it was supposed to end at midnight but I heard from the chef that the revelry continued after that. The boss was still making toasts for the success of Ukraine in its war with Russia until well past one a.m. The fundraiser was an outstanding success, and he was very happy about the amount of donations received."

Sean and Betty ordered their meals, both having steak-frites and sharing a bottle of red Rhone wine. They strolled along the waterfront afterward until it was time for Betty's ferry. They agreed to meet again soon and Sean promised to call to set it up.

*****

When Sean told what he'd learned the next day to Hamish, the latter shook his head. "That makes it impossible for Dimanche to be the one who asked at the restaurant for Seamus Dooley, and virtually impossible that he might have been involved in his killing. The drive from Halifax would take at least four hours. So I guess we're back to square one."

"That's what I thought. I've no reason to doubt what the waiter said. Who else might've been interested in seeing Dooley dead?"

"I don't know. I'm going to make another visit to Rothesay. I need to talk to Mary Carstairs, and I'd like to look through Dooley's house once again."

*****

Mary was wearing black and was looking drawn when she met him at the door of her father's house in Rothesay. "I guess I'll arrange for an estate sale of the contents. There's not much here except for his clothes, some beds, sofas, and a lawnmower in the garage. The F-150 was pretty much a write-off. I got the local garage, where it was towed, to buy it for $1,000. They'll try to get the engine running again, but, if not, the vehicle is still worth something to them for parts."

"If you don't mind, I'd like to have a look with you through his stuff. Maybe there's something we missed that might give me a clue as to why he was killed."

"Is it definitely murder now?"

"The circumstantial evidence is too strong against it being an accident. Given the tire tracks, it looks like his truck was parked near to where it went into the lake, and behind it was another vehicle. The police are investigating it as murder. It seems to me very likely that his death is related to what happened in Halifax five years ago that led him to hide here under an assumed name. However, I don't have a suspect. The person I thought might be involved has a very good alibi."

"That was so long ago, I thought it would just fade from people's memories, and he could start leading a normal life again. Actually, that's what he had succeeded in doing before you came along." She looked at him reproachfully. "It was your poking around that led to his death, wasn't it?"

Hamish hung his head. "I've had that argument with myself several times now, and each time I've had to admit that I must have triggered something that put him in harm's way. But I couldn't let sleeping dogs lie, not if it involved a major crime. Now I seem to have provoked a worse one! But I can't see why your father had to die. Why was he still a threat to them?" He shook his head sorrowfully.

"At least you seem to have put the police on their trail, so the criminals won't get off scot free this time. What made you dig up this old business at the Halifax restaurant where my father used to work?"

"That's what's so strange. It was because of a business dispute between a friend of mine, who runs a French restaurant near BistroDimanche. He hired me to investigate dirty tricks that he said the owner was playing on him. Then someone broke into the detective agency's office and stole the file I had on the owner of BistroDimanche. I still don't know why, though it may be related to his activities before he came to Canada. It's what set me off to investigate him further, and to discover more about his past."

Mary and Hamish started on the ground floor. She had hired cleaners to clean up, and replace her father's clothes and kitchen equipment in their proper places. "An outfit that does estate sales will have an open house next Saturday and Sunday. What doesn't sell, I'll give to charity. Then I'll put the house up for sale. There's a modest mortgage on the house, and after paying it off there should be a few tens of thousand dollars left. They'll go to my brother and me, since we're his sole heirs. I wanted to look through the house once again to remove any keepsakes and other personal stuff of my father's." She sniffed.

She put most of the items in the bathroom into a trash bin, but kept an ancient straight razor with a silver handle which had been passed down from her grandfather. From the master bedroom, she removed only a pair of spectacles and a cashmere jacket, leaving the rest of his clothes to be sold. She hesitated in front of a knife rack in the kitchen. "These are fine quality, but they're of no use to me. I'll let the estate sale people try to get the best price for them."

A quick look at the basement suggested that most of its contents should go to charities or be thrown into the trash bin. Hamish looked through the box of books. "I might enjoy this book on twentieth century European history. As he leafed through it, a newspaper clipping fell out. It was in German, a language Hamish didn't know, though he could read that it was from the May 11, 1991, issue of *Die Welt*. It included a photograph. Hamish casually examined it, then stared. "This is a photo of my friend, Des Stuart, in his army uniform! How did he happen to make it into an old German newspaper? Do you mind if I keep this, and the book as well?"

"Of course not, you're welcome to it. My father was a cook for the Canadian Forces based in Lahr, West Germany. That no doubt explains the clipping. When the base closed in the early 1990s, after the end of the Cold War, he returned to Canada."

"That's an interesting coincidence! Did he ever mention knowing Des? After all, his restaurant is very close to the BistroDimanche where your father worked."

"He never mentioned that name, or knowing someone in Halifax he'd met in Germany. In fact, he never talked very much about his time there. When he returned, he married my mother, and I was born a year later. Sadly, my mother died when I was still a teenager."

*****

Hamish's friend Izzie knew some German, so he asked her to translate the clipping from *Die Welt*.

"I won't try to translate it exactly, but the article says that squadron quartermaster-sergeant Desmond Stuart, attached to the British Army of the Rhine, was honoured for his service in West Germany at a gala dinner, before his departure to his home country. Attached is a photo of him in military uniform."

"I knew he had been a career soldier in the British military, but I didn't know his rank nor that he had served in Germany. If I recall, a quartermaster is an NCO whose responsibility is to provide food and lodging to the troops. Interesting …"

"It could just be what it seems, a bookmark, and it was only kept for that reason. Let me see the book itself."

Hamish passed her the book, *Europe After World War II.*

Izzie flipped through the index and table of contents. "The book has a lot of ground to cover. There are chapters on the Allied Occupation of Germany, the Cold War, European Economic Integration, the Dismantling of the Soviet Empire, German Reunification, and so forth. Do you know what page the clipping marked?"

"It was near the beginning of the chapter on the Cold War."

Izzie skimmed through the chapter. "Oh, here's a photo that shows Vladimir Putin in Dresden, where he was stationed by the KGB from 1985 to 1989. According to the caption, he's shown talking to his Stasi colleagues. The KGB was something of an older brother to the East German outfit, and both were involved in spying on the West Germans. Wait a minute … I think I recognize one of them. It looks like Serge Dimanche! I still have the photo I took at the UNICEF Gala. Let me look in my cell phone."

Hamish grabbed the book. "You're right! It looks like a younger, slimmer Serge Dimanche. So that must be the past that he was trying to hide! I wonder how much Janine knows of his background, if she met him in Paris, as she says."

"If Serge Dimanche was aware that Dooley had identified him as a former Communist spy, Serge might have a strong motive to kill him. But according to what you and Sean learned, he couldn't have been in Rothesay when the murder was committed."

"That newspaper clipping puts Desmond in Germany at roughly the same time as Dooley and Dimanche. I need to find out more about his involvement with them."

27

"Is that Hamish? It's Henri Faucher again. I just wanted to tell you another thing I learned about Serge Dimanche. I called my counterpart at the German BKA, the Federal Criminal Police Office, to find out if they had a file on him."

"Did they?"

"Yes and no. He was in fact a double agent, working both for the Stasi and the West German security services. He apparently saw the fall of the Berlin Wall coming, and managed to get out of the GDR before things got bad for the Stasi, and told what he knew to the West Germans and their NATO allies. After reunification he was given an official German passport in the name of Serge Dimanche, even though his real name was Sergei Demanchuk. At that point, the German intelligence services had no further use for Stasi double agents, and they facilitated his departure to France."

"That's amazing, Henri! So were the French intelligence services aware of this at the time?"

"I expect some people were, but the intelligence business is a curious one. Even if you are on the same side, there's still a great incentive to keep what you know to yourself. So the DGSI, with responsibility for France's internal security, was not informed by the DGSE, which was concerned with external threats, or by the German security services."

*****

Hamish filled Sean in about what he had learned from Faucher. "I thought all along that something was fishy about Serge Dimanche. Now I remember what was also in my trial notes that were stolen. One of the witnesses against Serge Dimanche, who worked as a waiter in BistroDimanche but had been dismissed the month before, pretended that Dimanche was a Stasi agent, and even gave what he claimed was his real name, Sergei Demanchuk. The defence said that was preposterous, and accused the man of making things up in retaliation for being fired. They asked that the testimony be stricken from the record, which I agreed to. In any case, it was irrelevant to the case against Dimanche."

Sean shook his head. "Wow, what a shocker! So Dimanche had a past that he was keen to hide. With his French name, he could hope not to be recognized. I'm not familiar with what went on in East Germany. I'm going to do some online research."

Hamish fixed himself a cup of coffee in the kitchen and came back to the agency's office.

Sean was at his computer, reading from an online history of East Germany. "It says here that the country, also known as the German Democratic Republic, or GDR–which existed only from 1949 to 1990–was at its end probably the world's most extreme example of a police state. Surveillance was carried out by a secret police organisation, the State Security Service, or Stasi. It was formed along the lines of the Soviet KGB, and effectively infiltrated every institution of East German society and daily life. It carried out its work both through its official apparatus and through a vast network of informants and unofficial collaborators."

"That sounds grim. I can't believe they got away with it!"

"Apparently, ordinary citizens spied on and denounced colleagues, friends, neighbours, and even family members. It says here that by 1989 the Stasi had over a million collaborators as well as a hundred thousand regular employees. It maintained files on approximately six million East German citizens—more than a third of the population. An attempt by Stasi workers to destroy those files after the fall of the Berlin Wall and the collapse of the regime was only partially successful."

"Oh, what happened to them, then?"

"Many of the files escaped destruction, and others were later reconstructed from torn documents. Apparently, that effort is still underway. I see that in the meantime an archive of Stasi files is open to those who have a legitimate reason for consulting them."

"I'm not sure that I would want to know."

"You're right. Many former GDR citizens have been devastated after learning that friends and relatives–even spouses–had denounced them to the Stasi."

Sean did some more searching and was now scanning down a screen of names. "It's a database of Stasi agents. After the fall of the Berlin wall. Stasi agents disappeared into the woodwork, but ordinary citizens who had been hounded by the Stasi identified many of them. I've come across a list of about eighty thousand alleged Stasi agents and informants, put together from individual testimonies and surviving records. The name Sergei Demanchuk is on that list."

Hamish scratched his nose. "So if Serge Dimanche is identified as Sergei Demanchuk, does that mean that he can be sued by his East German victims? After all, Stasi spied on GDR citizens, jailed and tortured them for innocent things, such as expressing an interest in emigrating or criticising the government."

"From what I've been able to find out by reading online articles, the German government after reunification has found it difficult to prosecute Stasi agents, because they were operating under a different system of laws. I read somewhere that even the head of Stasi, who was convicted by lower courts of various crimes, including ordering assassinations, was liberated by Germany's top court because he was working for a sovereign government at the time, the GDR, and Germany's laws do not apply retroactively to it. So Demanchuk might not be in legal jeopardy in Germany. After all, they gave him a new identity and sent him on his way. They don't want to see him again."

Hamish demurred. "I can understand that. But even so, Dimanche would want to hide from those GDR citizens whose lives were ruined by Stasi persecution. They might well attempt to wreak their revenge on a former agent. Revealing that he had been a Stasi agent would mean that he would perpetually have to look over his shoulder, since he might be in danger of assassination. I expect that he would do everything he could to avoid being called out. This might explain why he has no presence on social media and gives so few details about his past life."

28

Hamish called Desmond Stuart using WhatsApp. "I learned something interesting, Des. Serge Dimanche is not his real name, it's Sergei Demanchuk. Making that known might put a dent in the reputation of BistroDimanche as a purveyor of traditional French food. What do you think?"

"I don't know, Hamish. After all, I own an authentic French restaurant, but I make no claim to being French!"

"Exactly! But Dimanche does. So if it were widely known that he's a fraud, he wouldn't be able to do those impersonations of a Parisian bistro chef. You could hit back at him by leaking the fact that his name was changed from Sergei Demanchuk, and that he lied about being a native Frenchman. Oh, by the way, I came across a clipping from a German newspaper containing your photo. It said you were a non-commissioned officer in the British army, stationed in Germany around 1990. I had no idea!"

"Yes, I left the army shortly thereafter. The end of the Soviet Union meant that the British military's involvement in Germany could shrink, like those of other NATO countries, and I took early retirement. A few years later, I decided to move to

Canada. I have relatives here. To get back to Serge Dimanche, did you find out anything else about his activities?"

"One of his staff members at the restaurant was observed stealing expensive cuts of meat from the Atlantic Food Services truck. We notified the Halifax police and one of their agents was on the scene the following week in order to catch them in the act. Unfortunately, the police moved in too soon and didn't catch the thief pilfering the shipments. But at least now BistroDimanche won't try that again."

"So they were the ones who stole my food?"

"It appears so. Here's another thing I learned about Dimanche from one of my friends in Europe: He was a Stasi agent in East Germany before the fall of the Berlin Wall. "

"A Stasi agent! That's amazing! It also explains a lot. He has been using his surveillance skills to advantage, both against me and to rob his suppliers. I know a journalist, Tom Gallo, who writes a blog about local restaurants and things to do around Halifax. I'll feed him the information—he's no friend of Serge Dimanche. You're sure that his real name was Sergei Demanchuk, and that he's been identified as a former Stasi agent?"

"That's right. But I would think twice about revealing that information. It's bound to be disturbing. It might prompt a violent reaction on Dimanche's part."

*****

The next day Hamish checked the blog that Des had mentioned to him. Under "Local Restaurant News" was a post:

"Rumour has it that the real name of Serge Dimanche, the owner of the eponymous BistroDimanche chain, is in fact Sergei Demanchuk. Moreover, far from having learned his cooking at his French grandmother's stove, it seems that his early life was spent holding the feet of East Germans to the fire–literally! It has been revealed to us that the name Sergei Demanchuk is on a list of former Stasi agents. Apparently he cleared out of East Germany around the time of the fall of the Berlin Wall, made himself a new identity, and moved to France before coming to Canada. If only the dishes served at BistroDimanche restaurants showed the same inventiveness!"

*****

The voice on the phone sounded desperate. "Marjoree, it's awful the lies that they're spreading about my husband! Claiming that he's a former Stasi agent, and that his real name is not Serge Dimanche!"

"Please calm down, Janine. I'm sure that if it's not true, his denial will make them stop. He can sue them for defamation. Why don't you come by Ashcroft? Let's have lunch at the sailing club here. The food's pretty good. It'll take your mind off things."

"I guess so. I'm not doing myself any good by chewing this over. Are you free today? I can be there in half an hour, and meet you at noon. Is that OK?"

*****

The dimly-lit dining room had a nautical appearance, with ships' steering wheels, club burgees, and photos of famous sailboats, including the Bluenose, on the walls. The round tables were made of dark wood and each was surrounded by a foursome of chairs, of a similar construction and colour. Marjoree had chosen a table in a corner, and she waved to Janine when she saw her enter, looking distraught.

"Who is this awful Tom Gallo? Do you know him?"

"I think he's a friend of Desmond Stuart, who runs a restaurant that competes with BistroDimanche, called *Bord de l'eau*."

"Oh, Desmond. I see now. It's his way of getting back at Serge."

"Why would he want to do that?"

Janine paused to consider the question, and whether she wanted to answer it. She nodded her head, having decided what she had to do. "It all goes back to the time we knew each other in Germany. You've guessed that Serge is not a native French speaker. He did in fact defect from the GDR, shortly before the fall of the Berlin Wall and subsequent disintegration of the Soviet empire. He saw the writing on the Wall!" She laughed bitterly at her little joke. "I was attached to British intelligence. France was no longer in NATO but wanted to have some pieces in the chess game, and it retained some of its post-WWII responsibilities as an occupying allied power. I was good at languages and had a background in counter-espionage, so I was useful to the British. I was seconded by my employer, the DGSE, or the *Direction Générale de la Sécurité Extérieure*–the equivalent of Britain's MI6. I was stationed in Bielefeld. That's where I met Desmond, who was working at British Army HQ, though not in intelligence, but rather as a procurement officer. He was quite a dashing fellow then, and good company. We became close friends."

"So you've known him a long time!"

"Yes, actually I've known him longer than my husband. Serge and I met when he was debriefed–I should say interrogated–after fleeing the GDR. It didn't go well. Some of the MI6 agents doubted his *bona fides*. For them, Serge was still a Stasi functionary and was distrusted as a result. They questioned Serge's motives, and scoffed at the intelligence Serge provided. Some even favoured putting Serge on a train back to East Berlin, and having the regime hang him as a traitor. I argued strongly against doing this, and fortunately the West Germans wanted to have no part of that. In the end, Serge provided a host of useful details on the operations of the Stasi, and this helped West Germany secure their headquarters after the fall of the Wall and before their agents could destroy all the files."

"So how did you get to know Serge?"

"After his interrogation he was hung out to dry. The British and West Germans didn't know what to do with him, so they basically interned him in an old military camp. I visited him occasionally to check how he was doing, and tried to cheer him up. He was unhappy because he realized that he had contributed to the horrors of a bad regime, while at the same time he felt guilty about ratting out his comrades. I started to see him as a good person, though flawed, as we all are. In French we have a saying: *Comprendre, c'est tout pardonner.* Loosely translated, it means: Understanding is forgiving. I'm not sure you or I, if we had been in the GDR at the time, would have done differently."

"So how did he eventually get to leave the military camp and move to France?"

"After a few months, the Wall fell, and then reunification of the two parts of Germany became possible. The West German government preferred that the past be buried, since it didn't want tales of espionage and Stasi atrocities to put a spanner in the works. After all, they needed the permission of the wartime Allied governments to create a united Germany. So they were happy to get rid of Serge. By that time we were lovers, and we had wild plans to start a restaurant in Canada. I returned to the DGSE, but they wouldn't let me retire for another few years. So we lived in Paris until I could. Serge learned the restaurant trade, and we made plans for the future. Then we moved here."

"Wow, what a story! So you were an intelligence agent. Are you still in touch with Desmond? Do you think he's still fond of you?"

"Possibly, but he's never tried to get in touch. Desmond resents our success with the restaurants here. He never actually met Serge in Germany nor was told what he had done, though he knew of his existence and was jealous of him. Serge dislikes Desmond because *Bord de l'eau* is more upscale than BistroDimanche. They're bitter rivals in the restaurant business. That's why Serge tried to sabotage *Bord de l'eau,* and Desmond leaked information about Serge's past. Serge also suspects that the waiter that he hired away from *Bord de l'eau* was in fact a deliberate plant on Desmond's part, in order to implicate BistroDimanche in the thefts of food from AFS."

"What about Seamus Dooley, the former chef of the Halifax BistroDimanche? Did you know him in Germany as well? He was working at Canada's Lahr air force base. Apparently he's been found dead in New Brunswick, and the police are suspicious that it may be due to foul play."

"No, I wasn't aware he had been in Germany. I met with him in his role as the chef at our Halifax restaurant, but nothing more. I haven't seen or heard from him for more than five years. I can't think of why Serge or Desmond would care about him after all this time."

"Well, someone seems to have felt threatened by him. Apparently, he had an article about Desmond from a German newspaper in his house, and a book with a photo of Serge indicating that he was a Stasi agent in it."

"Can I see it? I'm curious."

"I'll mention it to Hamish and Sean. I don't have the book with me. Tell me, what was Serge's reaction to the leak about his past?"

"He's mad as hell, and he's sure that this is Desmond's way of getting back at him. I don't know what he'll do. I'm worried."

29

"Marjoree, did Janine really admit to being with British intelligence in Germany?" Hamish asked. "If so, that certainly puts a new complexion on things. I guess that blog post by Tom Gallo has set the cat among the pigeons! It's significant that Desmond apparently didn't know that Serge had an earlier life as a Stasi agent. Otherwise, he would probably have revealed Serge's identity earlier. It's pretty clear that he would do anything to get at his rival. I wonder now if some of the sabotage he accuses Serge of doing is fabricated. I think we've been used by Desmond to get at Serge."

Marjoree, Hamish and Sean were sitting around the table in the office, each with a cup of coffee. She nodded. "Janine felt she had to reveal things about the past, even though her first impulse was to deny that the allegations about Serge were true. She's worried about what comes next. Are Serge and Desmond going to escalate their war?"

Sean interjected: "I wonder what Serge's reaction will be when he learns that Janine has talked to you, Marjoree. But you've got to show her that German news story. She may be able to solve the mystery of Seamus Dooley's role in all of this."

*****

Janine and Marjoree met this time for lunch at the LaHave Bakery. Janine had some things to do at the BistroDimanche office in Bridgewater, so she suggested the venue, which was one of her favourites. The little rooms of the restaurant were crowded, as usual, and the two women chose their food at the counter from the limited menu posted on a chalkboard.

"Let me have a look at that article before they bring us our food," Janine said. "Hmm, Desmond looks the way I remember him–though I'll bet he's changed quite a bit over the past 30 years! It was somewhat unusual to have a German newspaper comment on the departure of a foreign soldier. But there's nothing there that we don't already know. I think that the significance of the article is that it indicates that Seamus knew Desmond at the time. It might also be worth your while to look carefully at the book where it served as a bookmark."

*****

Marjoree reported back to Hamish and Sean about her lunch with Janine, returning the history book and the newspaper clipping. "I'm afraid that she didn't find anything in the article that can help us. But at her suggestion I looked carefully at the book itself, and I think I've discovered something that may be useful, in addition to the photo of Sergei Demanchuk in Dresden with Vladimir Putin: a slip of paper that was inserted in the book's spine. It wasn't visible until I put the book on a flat surface and splayed the pages. Then I noticed the slip behind the binding, and I removed it with tweezers. It lists 'payments received from D'. Beside various dates, it gives amounts of $250 or $500.

All the dates are around the time of Serge's fraud trial, before Seamus disappeared."

"Great work, Marjoree! These may be the payments from Dimanche that Seamus mentioned to me in Rothesay."

"There's also a 10-digit number scribbled below the figures. It starts with 902 so I assume it's a Halifax phone number. "

"Let's try the number to see if it's still in service," Hamish suggested. The phone rang at the other end. As Hamish was about to hang up, he heard a recorded message: "For reservations at *Bord de l'eau*, please press one, …" Hamish hung up, frowning. "So it's not Serge Dimanche's phone after all! I wonder why Seamus had Des's phone number. Perhaps he was hoping to get a job at *Bord de l'eau* at the time, since by then he had left BistroDimanche? We may never know, now that Seamus is dead, but I'll ask Des the next time I see him."

30

Hamish and Izzie had decided to have a fancy night out, and decided on *Bord de l'eau* for their dinner meal. Desmond promised to let them choose from a special menu. The chef, who was from Languedoc and looked like a rugby player, with a body like a side of beef and a thick face with a broken nose, came out from the kitchen wearing his apron to chat with them. "If you like duck I have a marvellous *confit* which I import from France. Or if you like dishes from the *sud-ouest* I can offer you a *bourride*. Otherwise a *filet de sole à la normande*–very fresh, in a cream sauce with mushrooms and small shrimp. To start, I have some *crevettes à l'anchoïade* or a *bisque de homard.*"

Izzie chose the *bisque* and the *bourride*, Hamish the *crevettes* and the *sole*, and they settled on a white Languedoc wine.

Desmond came back to talk to them as they were waiting for their first course, bringing three small glasses of Banyuls. It was early, and the dining room was not yet crowded. "Here's to you both! I hope you enjoy your meal." He pulled out a chair from an empty table and sat down, taking a sip from his glass. "May I join you for a few minutes? Let me thank you for all the info you gave me on Serge Dimanche. Hopefully now he will keep out of my business! Revealing him to be Sergei Demanchuk will have put him off his game."

Hamish took a few seconds before replying, with a sardonic smile: "I think you were pulling my leg, Des, about not knowing Dimanche's background. Marjoree is friends with Janine, who filled us in. Apparently, you knew both Serge and her in Germany back in the late 1980s. An article in a German newspaper kept by Seamus Dooley confirms that you were there. Did you know him as well?"

The other man looked away. In a halting voice he said, "Yes, that's true. I did know them all. Janine and I were good friends but she fell in love with Serge. I never learned much about him, never met him. I hired you because I wanted more information about his background, as well as to find out whether Dimanche was now trying to sabotage me. I thought Dimanche was trying to ruin my business because his own was in trouble. He probably thought he could stay afloat if mine went under because he'd have less competition. With the Covid pandemic, many restaurants can no longer make a profit. We've become desperate rivals over a slice of a shrinking pie."

"What about Dooley? What do you think happened to him?"

"I don't know. I haven't talked to him in years."

"Did you put him up to accusing Dimanche of serving contraband liquor? Maybe he decided at the last moment that he didn't want to perjure himself, and he decided to disappear."

"No, no! It was Dimanche's doing. He bought Dooley's silence." Desmond finished his glass and got up, his usual genial expression replaced by a frown. "I've got to go, there are some arrangements I have to make. Enjoy your meal." He stalked back to his kitchen.

Izzie turned to Hamish and said in a whisper: "He certainly was getting excited. Did you believe what he said?"

"Not completely. There's something that doesn't quite fit. I'm going to talk to Dimanche. I need his side of the story–if he'll tell it to me."

The meal was as tasty as they expected. They paid their bill and left, not having seen Desmond again. It was a cool but dry evening, and they enjoyed the view out over the harbour. A well-lit-up freighter passed in front of them on its way out to sea. They turned and walked a few blocks to the Neptune Theatre to see a play for which Izzie had bought tickets, and afterward returned to her apartment.

31

Hamish drove back along the gravel road to the Dimanche mansion from Chester, and parked in its circular drive. It was a glorious late summer day, and a light breeze off the water gave a welcome freshness to the air. Serge answered the bell, and looked quizzically at Hamish, whom he recognized from the UNICEF Gala.

"Hello again. Sorry to drop in uninvited, but I'd like to hear your side of the story. Is it OK if I come in?"

Dimanche hesitated. "I guess so. Why don't you come through to the patio. It's nicer there than inside."

The patio had a round black iron table with matching chairs. Serge commented that they often ate dinner outside in summer. The rest of the patio had some lounge chairs, and he motioned for Hamish to sit in one of them, then he sat in another that was next to it.

He gazed down the lawn to his dock with a sigh, then reluctantly turned to face Hamish. "So, what would you like to know about?"

"Who are you? Is it true that you are really Sergei Demanchuk?"

He frowned, taken aback by the abruptness of the question. "I was. I legally changed my name when I defected to West Germany. My ancestry is Ukrainian. My parents fled Ukraine to Germany after the Nazis retreated following the Soviet victory at Stalingrad. I was born in the Soviet occupation zone of Germany."

"So you grew up in the GDR. How did you become a Stasi agent?"

"After the war, my parents lived in poverty, scarcely able to afford food to put on the table. It was a terrible period across much of Europe, but especially in Soviet occupied territories. I was lucky because I did well in school. I was good at languages, and when I left high school and did my military service, I was able to get a place at the Stasi training college. I learned Russian and French, as well as some English, and was training to become one of their foreign agents–a spy, if you like."

"You believed the Soviet propaganda?"

"Not at all! In the GDR, you were either a spy, or someone who was spied on. The only way to have a life was to be the former. Given my training, I studied ways of obtaining foreign intelligence, in preparation for the day I would be sent to the West. They hoped to have me implanted in some government department, like Guillaume, the assistant to Willy Brandt who brought down the West German government after he was unmasked as a Stasi agent."

"You were smuggled across the border to the West?"

"I was given false papers identifying me as a resident of West Germany. Obviously, given the common language, there was no easy way to distinguish between an East and a West German."

"But were you caught? You ended up talking to West German intelligence."

"I just wanted to escape the GDR. Fortunately I had convinced my Stasi superiors that I was trustworthy. As soon as I got out, I contacted the NATO authorities, and I told the West Germans, the Americans, and the British what I knew about the GDR. I was lucky, I guess, that soon after that the East German regime collapsed, so there was no one to come after me and kill me."

"And you and Desmond Stuart knew each other?"

"We never met. I was interrogated at Bielefeld, and he was stationed there. We both knew Janine. That was all."

"What was the reason for your rivalry?"

Serge shrugged. "He had his sights on Janine, and she chose me instead."

Hamish paused for a moment, then continued. "OK, now tell me what happened five years ago, when Seamus Dooley was supposed to testify against you at my trial, but didn't?"

"I've been trying to work this out for myself. I think Desmond must have bribed Seamus to testify against me. I wasn't using contraband liquor. I admit that I refilled name bottles of gin, vodka, or whisky with cheaper, but legal, booze–most bars and restaurants do that. Seamus quit because he wanted to choose his own menus, and do his own purchasing of food. Janine and I thought that we should keep the same menu so people would know what to expect, and it made economic sense for procurement to be centralized at our Bridgewater head office. As a result of that I think Dooley developed a grudge against me. He probably went to see Desmond about a chef's job. I'm guessing that Desmond suggested that he accuse me of something more serious, and that he agreed to do it. I admit that I was desperate to stop him from testifying. I offered money to him if he skipped out, and he took it. That's the last I heard of him."

"So who killed him, if it wasn't you? You didn't go to New Brunswick to find him?"

"I certainly did not. I think you should talk to your friend Desmond about that."

Hamish didn't reply. Instead, he tried to digest what Dimanche had said. It seemed to ring true. "I'll talk to Desmond. There's more to this than meets the eye."

32

Sam O'Leary was speaking with Hamish on the phone. "Too bad the tires of Serge Dimanche's car can't be proven to be the same as those on the car whose tire prints were found near to the fatal accident. Now you say that Dimanche was almost certainly not the person who visited Dooley's restaurant in Rothesay and asked for him. Are there any other suspects?"

"I know that Desmond Stuart, who owns the *Bord de l'eau* restaurant, also has a black SUV. In his case, it's an Audi. You might want to see if it has new Continental tires with the same tread. He's another person who was involved with Seamus Dooley in the past, and who has been an enemy of Dimanche for decades."

"You know, Judge, we did a little investigating of those complaints that Desmond Stuart made of vandalism at his restaurant. It turns out that the store across the street has security cameras that film that part of the street. And they show that guy Stuart outside, throwing red paint at his front door, so we're considering charging him with making a false statement to the police. We'll check out his car. Of course, if they match it won't prove that the tire prints we have are his, since the tires at the scene were new."

*****

"You're right, Judge, Desmond Stuart's car has the same Continental tires. But as I say, it just means that he's a suspect, it doesn't prove that he offed Seamus Dooley."

"Could you impound his car, and search for any evidence that Dooley was in the car? The way I see it, a pair of thugs kidnapped him in his house, and then drove him and the truck to Lake Dolan. Now, Dooley might have driven the truck, while one of them held a gun to his head, or he might have been compelled to ride in the SUV while the other thug drove the truck. Maybe tied up, or unconscious. But one way or another, his DNA might be in the SUV. I know it's a long shot, but maybe it's worth looking for."

"Well, we'll need to convince a judge to give us a search warrant. But what do we have? Not much linking Stuart to either the flight of a witness five years ago, or to a murder several hundred kilometres away from where he lives. I don't think that's going to work."

"OK, let me see if I can dig something up. By the way, do we know anything about the chef at *Bord de l'eau* restaurant? I gather he's French. I wonder how long he's been in Canada, and whether he's a permanent resident here."

"Let me look into that."

*****

Hamish called Dooley's daughter once again. "Mary, I'd like you to look through any letters or papers you might have from your father that might shed some light on his relations with

Desmond Stuart in Germany or here in Canada–or with Serge Dimanche, for that matter. Can you do that for me?"

"Sure. I'll look, but I can't think of anything off-hand. All this happened before I was born, so it's not something he would have written to me about."

"Why don't you have another look at his house. His personal papers must be there somewhere."

*****

Sean and Hamish were in the office at eight o'clock in the morning, each with his first cup of coffee.

"As I look back to my conversations with Desmond when I was still a judge, I remember he was particularly interested in the trial of Serge Dimanche. I would often go to *Bord de l'eau* for lunch, and by that time Desmond and I were friends, so I would chat with him about what went on in my court that morning. He asked me about the witness, Seamus Dooley, and wanted to know when he would testify. I don't know what I said, but I think he must have guessed that there was some doubt whether Dooley would show up, since the police had not been able to contact him. I told him that we might be able to locate him through his daughter. I'd forgotten her name, but I probably jotted it down in my trial notes. However, that was a dead end too, probably because we didn't have her married name."

"Is it possible that Des remembered the conversation, and thought he could find Dooley if he had his daughter's name? Could he have hired someone to steal your trial notes?"

"But why now, and not five years ago? And why did Des hire me two months ago? He said it was because he suspected that Serge was playing dirty tricks on him. But the opposite seems to have been true: he was playing dirty tricks on BistroDimanche. It may be that it's *Bord de l'eau* that is in financial trouble, and Des is trying to force his competition out of business."

"That may be, but what would getting your trial notes do to help? Could it be that Serge stole them instead?"

"I think both of them had something to fear if Dooley turned up. I don't expect that whoever hired a burglar to break into our office had that in mind. They may have wanted to ensure that those notes would never lead us to track Dooley down. So they stole them and burned them. Serge feared Dooley would testify against him about the liquor violations, while Dooley could accuse Desmond of bribing a witness to give false testimony. Moreover, if Dooley were arrested, he might well be forced to explain how he had known Desmond in Germany, and testify to their fraudulent billing of Canadian and British forces there. So Desmond did not want him found, or if he turned up, wanted to make him disappear."

"And how are you going to find who actually murdered Dooley?"

"I have my ideas … But you'll have to help me."

*****

The office phone rang, and Marjoree took the call. "It's Sam O'Leary, Hamish, wanting to talk to you."

"Hello, Sam, any luck?"

"I did find out a few things about your Desmond. He did indeed come to Canada in the mid-1990s, and became a permanent resident. He gave Seamus Dooley as one of his Canadian sponsors."

"So the two of them were close confederates after all. Anything else?"

"You asked me about his chef. Roland Lepage is on a temporary work permit. I tried to track down his activities in France but without success. I'd have to make a formal request to Citizenship and Immigration, and they would then contact their French counterparts. It could take months."

After hanging up, Hamish turned to Sean. "I'll bet you the chef at *Bord de l'eau* was a rugby player. Why don't you try searching for his name on the internet. Let's see what comes up."

"Here's an article in the French newspaper *Midi Libre* that mentions a rugby match between Béziers and Carcassonne in which a certain Roland Lepage scored the winning try. And there's another from two years ago where his retirement from professional rugby is announced, following his conviction for assault and battery. A confrontation with a fan of another team led to a fight in which Lepage beat his opponent to a pulp. Do you think this is the guy? But so what?"

"It sounds as though Desmond's chef doesn't shrink from violence."

33

"Hamish, this is Mary Carstairs. I've been looking through some papers I retrieved from my father's house, and I found something that might be of interest to you. It's a list of food suppliers to the kitchens at the Lahr Canadian Forces base in Germany. My father apparently did the food procurement for the entire base. The list includes the name of Desmond Stuart. It appears that they were in touch with each other in Germany, and perhaps there was some sharing of supplies between British and Canadian forces–I don't know."

"That's interesting. Is there anything else you found that gives more details of their relations there? And what about his service records or old passports? Did he keep any of those? Do you have precise dates of when he was in Germany, and when he was discharged? Did he talk to you about his life there when you were growing up?"

"Unfortunately I don't have more information on his time in Germany. When he returned to Canada he married my mother, who lived here in New Brunswick, and I was born in 1995. He was never keen on talking about his life in Germany. My mother died when I was eighteen. At the time, I was at university in

Saint John, while my father was working in Digby. I married James Carstairs when I was twenty-two, but we divorced three years later. So I haven't been living with my father for some years now."

"I wonder what happened to his documents. I'm guessing that he might have put things in a safety deposit box. Is that possible?"

"Maybe, but I don't know where the key might be. I'll go back to the house to look tomorrow. Fortunately the estate sale isn't until this Saturday."

"I could come and help you look. Shall we meet there at around noon?"

"Sure, that would be fine."

*****

Hamish made an early start and with light traffic got to the house in Rothesay a little after twelve. Mary's car was already parked in front of the house. Hamish rang the bell, then let himself in. The door was unlocked. He shouted from the entryway. "Mary, where are you?"

When he heard nothing he pushed open the door and entered the living room. There were boxes strewn across the floor. He called again, worried now.

She emerged from a bedroom carrying a box full of papers and knick-knacks. "I think I found some of the things you were looking for. I guess I missed it the first time, since it just looked like junk. But at the bottom of the box there are some envelopes and files."

They went to the kitchen and she laid the contents of the box out on the counter. "Here's my father's birth certificate, marriage licence, and a statement of pension benefits upon his discharge from the Canadian forces. And there's a note with the letterhead of British Forces Germany. It seems to concern an arrangement for supplying foodstuffs to the Canadian air base at Lahr." Mary passed the documents to Hamish.

She rifled through the remaining papers. "Oh, here's something that might interest you. It's a letter signed by Desmond Stuart. It says: 'As agreed, payment for invoiced supplies is to be accompanied by a 5 percent premium for administrative expenses to be paid in cash.'"

"Let me take the two letters about the provisioning of Lahr. I'll go see Desmond Stuart to find out what he has to say about them."

They rooted through the other boxes, but did not find any more documents nor a safety deposit key. They did find a model of the Avro Arrow in one of the boxes, and her father's General Services Medal.

*****

Hamish stopped at the police station in Rothesay, on the off chance that Jeremy Lepreau might be in. He was in luck. "Constable, is there any chance some local security camera might have filmed a black SUV with Nova Scotia plates going by? We have two suspects whose car tires match the prints found at the scene of Seamus Dooley's drowning. It's a long shot, but it might be that we can spot one of the two in the area at about the time it took place. You could try to get photos of cars at or close to the Gastropub, and between the restaurant and Dooley's house."

"Sure, I'll look into it. They will probably have taken Route 1 down from the Trans-Canada, so I can check with the RCMP about cameras along that route."

"You might also ask about video footage at the toll plazas on the Cobequid Pass section of the Trans Canada between Masstown and Thomson Station. I suspect that they will have cameras to catch those from out of province evading the toll, even if a car with Nova Scotia plates would not have to pay it."

34

Sean was in Jeff Winding's office. Beth was explaining her theory of access to the AFS database of orders and deliveries. "I think the problem is with those sophisticated scanners that your drivers use to record the deliveries. They're identical to the ones used at the warehouse, where the things added and removed from inventory are recorded. If someone got a hold of one, they could read what was in our database. I think that's what happened with the stolen steaks. The thieves didn't have someone inside the warehouse, or a surveillance camera. It was much more straightforward–they used a scanner in a way that authorized them access to our computer system. I'm guessing that the driver who quit after two months was deliberately planted to get a hold of one."

Jeff seemed sceptical. "What do you think, Sean? Could that explain it?"

"After looking at what that handheld scanner can do, I realize that Beth is right. It could well be the way someone got advanced knowledge of where to find the food they wanted to steal. What you need to do is to try to track down the driver who quit and didn't return his scanner."

"We tried the address and phone number he gave as his contact information, but no one knew of him at that address, and the number wasn't in service."

"What about references? Maybe one of them will know something more about him."

"I'll dig out the application and let you know."

The meeting broke up. On his way out of the building, Sean ran into Beth, whose office was down a corridor from Jeff Winding's. He smiled at her. "Are you happy now? Your boss has taken your contribution seriously."

"Maybe so, but there's no way I can get more responsibility here. Staff assistant is as senior a position as I can hope for. This place sucks! I'd much rather be a detective," she said shyly. "Want to discuss it over dinner? It's past five o'clock and I'm knocking off work now."

Sean looked at her longingly. "Sounds good to me. Know a good restaurant nearby?"

"The Canteen on Portland is a great place, and it's not far away. Let's do it!"

The modest-looking restaurant was on a sloping street with a short flight of steps leading up to the entrance. A terrace fronted on the sidewalk, but was accessed from inside. They got a table for two there. Sean was impressed by the eclectic menu. When they got their dishes, a scallop and pea risotto for Sean and a chowder for Beth, they hungrily dug into their food.

"Delicious," Sean said. "Now about detective work: it's pretty boring stuff most of the time, but other times we get dangerous assignments. I was once abducted at gunpoint, knocked unconscious and would have gone over a cliff if Hamish hadn't come along and saved me!"

"Wow, sounds rad! Can I get a job at your detective agency? I'm sure I could learn the ropes quickly, I'm a fast learner."

"I'll raise it with Hamish. In the meantime, do you want to take up where we left off?" Sean smiled lasciviously.

After finishing their meal they wandered back to her apartment arm in arm.

*****

The next day, Sean was back in Ashcroft when he got a call from Jeff Winding. "Sean, I checked with shipping, who did the hiring, and they admit that they didn't contact any of the references the fellow gave. They did check his driver's licence to make sure that he had a commercial permit, but that was all. I guess they didn't confirm that the address on the licence was the same as the phony address given by the driver they hired, whose name was Joe Arbullo."

"What references did he give?"

"Just one, a certain Juergen Bell, who runs a trucking company in the North End. I tried the number given on the form, but it's out of service. So I called the number given on the company's website and spoke to him. He denies all knowledge of Joe Arbullo or of having any of his drivers leave during the past year."

"So, it sounds as though this Joe Arbullo, or whatever his name is, deliberately gave false information when applying for a job at AFS–probably in order to steal one of your scanners."

"Sure looks like it. And he didn't leave a trail."

"But unless he had a forged licence, that should be his real name, and the Registry of Motor Vehicles will have some of these details. I'll ask my partner, Hamish Cameron, whether he has a contact there who can look into it. I'll get back to you as soon as I hear."

When he hung up the phone, he looked up and noticed Marjoree looking at him. "Sean, you slept over again in Halifax, didn't you? Do you expect to continue doing this without my commenting on it? Well, I'm not going to sit by and let you amuse yourself with another woman. It's that Beth, isn't it? I can see that you get all mushy whenever her name comes up!"

Sean hung his head. "OK, Marjoree, I admit that I've been seeing her. We should have had this conversation before. I shouldn't have kept you in the dark. I think I'm in love."

"At your age! And how old is she? From her voice on the phone I'd guess at least 15 years younger! Anyway, I'm not going to stand for it! You can find another assistant." She stormed out.

*****

Hamish took Marjoree's side. "Be reasonable, Sean! However attractive Beth is, it's not going to work between you and her. It's going to just be a brief coupling. Then you'll want to come back to Marjoree, and she won't have you. Think it over. Oh, and by the way, the guy I know at the Registry for Motor Vehicles says that Joe Arbullo lives in the North End, and his previous employer was the *Bord de l'eau* restaurant."

"What? So it's Desmond who's behind this hijacking of AFS! This doesn't make any sense. I tracked the truck and witnessed someone at BistroDimanche going through the delivery boxes. That, and the free drink offered by the restaurant seemed pretty conclusive. Could it be that the scanner was not used to do the thefts? I've got to talk to this guy Arbullo. Give me the address you have for him."

35

Sean drove from Ashcroft to Halifax's North End, to a modest house on Leeds Street. It was after five o'clock, so he thought he might catch Arbullo at home. The yard was devoid of vegetation, except for a large maple tree in front of the house and a lawn spotted with dandelions.

Sean rang the bell. A muscular man wearing jeans and a tee shirt, who looked to be in his forties, came out onto the stoop after half a minute and closed the door. "Yeah?"

"Are you Joe Arbullo?"

"That's right. What about it?"

"You worked for a couple of months as a driver for AFS in Bedford. What did you do with their scanner that reads barcodes? They've sent me to get it back."

"Well, I don't have it any more."

"You realize that it's an expensive item, and they reported it stolen. So you can expect the cops to come and search your house unless you find it."

"Now wait a minute! I can't help it if it disappeared. I just ain't got it."

"If you can't come up with it, then the police will get involved."

"OK, OK, I'll try to find it. If I do, I'll call AFS to let them know. How's that?"

"Make it quick. They aren't going to wait forever."

Sean went back to his car, which was parked nearby. He drove around the block and parked on a cross street where he could observe Arbullo's house. After ten minutes, the man came out, got in a Chevy Bolt, and drove off. Sean waited half a minute before following him. He saw him turn onto Massachusetts Avenue. Keeping well back, he tailed him down to Water Street and saw him park near the *Bord de l'eau* restaurant. Arbullo got out of his car and went into the restaurant.

Sean parked his car and waited. After a few minutes, the man came out carrying a piece of electronic equipment. *Looks like the scanner*, Sean thought. He got out of the car and trotted over to where the other man was about to get into his Chevy. Pulling out his phone, he took a picture of Arbullo and the scanner.

The man looked up, frightened. "Here, take the scanner and leave me alone! I did what you asked and located it. You can return it to AFS."

"So you and Desmond Stuart are in cahoots. What else have you conspired to do?"

Arbullo wrenched open his car door, got in, and slammed it in Sean's face. With a screech of tires he drove off, narrowly missing Sean who was standing on the pavement.

*****

"Sean, It's looking more and more as if Des is up to his eyeballs in ripping off AFS. But why would he do this? Is it to get the free food or to pin it on BistroDimanche? Or maybe both? I don't know if we can get any more evidence on this. I'm going to have to confront him, and hope he gives something away."

"That sounds dangerous. You can't do it alone."

"I'm going to talk to Sam O'Leary about this, to see if he can help out here."

36

Gottfried

The man examined the long row of apple trees behind the dilapidated barn. A scrub pine forest surrounded the farm, which was located on a back road ten kilometres from the Annapolis Basin. The white clapboard farmhouse dated back to the early years of the previous century. It had seen better days. Paint was peeling off the siding and window frames, and the roof looked as if it needed work. However, the house still kept out the rain and cold. A thin plume of wood smoke rose from the chimney now.

He picked one apple and bit into it. It was crisp, as an Empire should be. *Time to harvest them. I'll take the apples to the farmers' market in Annapolis Royal on Saturday. In the meantime, I'd better call the grocery store to make sure that they'll take some of them, as well as my leeks, broccoli, and cauliflower. I can stop there on my way to the farmers' market.*

Gottfried had been a clerk in a bank in Leipzig in what was then East Germany, with a wife and a young daughter. At work, he had imprudently confided his hopes that the GDR might loosen up its tyrannical regime. A colleague from work informed on him. The Stasi concluded that he was a traitor who was plotting the overthrow of the government. As a result, he lost his accountant's position and his family. He survived only by doing odd jobs on farms and stealing food.

The fall of the Berlin Wall came too late to allow him to resume his former life. After the reunification of East and West Germany, he was eligible for compensation by the government for the actions of the Stasi, causing him to lose his job unfairly. However, he could not provide the German authorities with proof of the actions taken by the Stasi against him that was required for him to qualify. With no prospects in the country, he chose to emigrate. Canada accepted his application to become a resident, and he had been fortunate to start a new life there. He moved to Nova Scotia because he had heard that farms in the Annapolis Valley were looking for agricultural labourers.

He worked for other farmers for a few years, and had saved enough to purchase a run-down farm. The farm had been abandoned after the death of the previous owner some years before, so the price was cheap. At present he grew blueberries and apples, as well as vegetables, and sold them locally.

He did all the hard work of tending the crops and marketing them by himself, because he could not afford to hire anyone. He gazed around at his property with satisfaction. He was proud of what he had achieved, little by little planting new apple trees when he could save enough to buy them from a nursery. The farming life was hard, but it gave him pleasure to build up a homestead, he who had been homeless for so long. However, memories of his past life in East Germany kept intruding on his happiness. He could not rid his mind of the evil that the Stasi had inflicted on him decades before.

He got out his collection of bushel baskets and a ladder from the barn and stuck them in the back of his beat-up truck. He left the truck next to the first tree in the row, in preparation for the harvest. Inside the house, he checked the week's weather forecast; it should be dry and sunny. He decided that tomorrow he would start picking the apples.

Since this year's harvest of apples seemed likely to exceed the amount he could sell locally, he looked online for other retailers of organic fruits and vegetables. By chance, he came across Tom Gallo's blog. Scrolling through the topics concerning food marketing, he came to the buzz about Halifax restaurants. He read with amazement and dismay the story concerning Bistro-Dimanche and the past life as Stasi agent of its owner, Serge Dimanche. Pounding his fist on the table, he screamed, *I'll kill him!*

The news had upended his life, reviving the furor that he harboured against the Stasi. During the next few days, he learned what he could about Serge Dimanche: where he lived, recent photos of him, the locations of his restaurants, and the name of his wife. He stopped picking his apples to make time to search the internet. When he thought he had exhausted that source of information, he went back to his apples, and sold what he could to his local contacts and at the Annapolis Royal market. Then he went back to planning how he was going to kill Dimanche.

First, he drove the hundred kilometres to Bridgewater, and sat in his beat up old truck while waiting to catch a glimpse of Dimanche. The day was rainy, and there were few pedestrians or autos on the street. No one went in or came out of the BistroDimanche office, nor was there a car parked nearby. He was getting hard looks from people walking by, and he gave up. From there, he drove to Chester and located the private road leading to the Dimanche residence. A quick look around convinced him that it was useless to park and wait, he would only draw attention to himself. However, he noticed the sailboat docked behind the house and decided that the easiest way to approach him might be from the water. He returned to his farm, regretting the expense of gasoline, but satisfied with the information he had gleaned.

An old Enfield rifle and some .303 shells had been in the barn when he purchased the farm. He had learned how to shoot when he had done his military service in the GDR decades before. Like riding a bicycle, it was not something that you forgot. He put a row of tin cans on a low stone wall that separated the house from the farmland behind. He made sure the rifle was in working condition and tried to hit one of the tin cans from twenty metres away. The first two shots went wide, but the third hit home. For the next two days, he practiced shooting at the targets. His aim got better and better. *That's enough practicing. I need to save enough ammunition to do what I have to do.*

He drove back to Chester with a small sailing dinghy in the truck's cargo bed. He had found it a few months before, beached along the Annapolis Basin. He thought it must have slipped its mooring as a result of the strong tidal currents in the basin combined with a spell of gale-force winds. *Someone didn't tie her up securely. Well, it's finders, keepers! I just hope I can figure out how to sail it to Dimanche's house.* He hid the rifle in some burlap bags which he stuffed under the sailboat's coaming.

Chester had a public boat ramp. Normally, boats were launched from a trailer, but Gottfried was able to drag the small boat out of his truck and slide it into the water. He tied up the boat to the launch dock and went back to his truck to get the mast, which he inserted into its hole in the sailboat's deck, and then he secured it to the mast step. *This is going easily so far. I hope the wind stays in the east so I can sail the five kilometres to Dimanche's house.* He unrolled the mainsail and cast off.

The wind was gusty, and at first he had trouble keeping the boat from heeling over. Once he got away from shore, he lowered the centreboard, which helped. He experimented with the mainsail, tightening it and letting it flap until he found the right setting. The boat was gliding smoothly through the water now. He steered the boat around an island with a thick stand of pine trees and headed west toward Dimanche's house. He had located it on Google maps and knew how to get there. He just had to follow the shoreline now until he reached it. It was the last house on the road, which was dead-ended there, so he thought he should be able to spot Serge Dimanche's mansion.

Now he was in the lee of the island and the trees blocked the wind, so the boat was nearly becalmed. *I should have brought a paddle, but it's too late now.* Little by little, the boat drifted until it was far enough from the island that it picked up the wind once again. In another half hour he was in sight of Dimanche's house. It was easily recognizable from the water because of the large sailboat docked behind it. He steered the boat toward an island opposite to it, furled the sail, and tied up to a branch that extended out over the water from a large fir tree. Turning now to examine the house, he spotted a figure sitting in a deck chair on the patio behind it. He got out his rifle and took careful aim.

37

Desmond

Hamish drove north, taking about half an hour to cover the 40 kilometres from Ashcroft-by-the-Sea to Desmond's house in Upper Tantallon. Desmond lived on a quiet, wooded road located about 30 kilometres southwest from his restaurant in the centre of Halifax. Hamish parked in the gravel driveway and rang the bell. Desmond Stuart answered the door, his face registering surprise and alarm at seeing Hamish there. With a forced smile, he said, "This is an unexpected pleasure, Hamish. Is anything the matter?"

"Sorry to barge in on you like this, Des, but I think we need to have a serious discussion about your relations with Seamus Dooley and Serge Dimanche. Can I come in?"

They sat in the living room, which was furnished with well-worn upholstered furniture, and a large entertainment centre sporting a big-screen TV. Hamish took one of the armchairs and

Desmond sat on a couch, facing him. "Why, what's up? Have you discovered some new information about them?"

Hamish met his gaze. "About them, and about you. You haven't exactly been forthcoming concerning your activities in Germany or here in Canada, have you, Des?"

"What do you mean?"

"You never mentioned to me when I was a judge trying Serge Dimanche for fraud that you had known him in Germany, and also the chief witness against him, Seamus Dooley. You pumped me for information about them. More recently, you hired me to discover whether he was sabotaging your restaurant, but that was all a ruse. You were the one sabotaging him."

Stuart shook his head. "That's not true! Dimanche was sabotaging me!"

"Then why was it you, not he, who splashed paint on your restaurant's door? Halifax police have surveillance camera pictures that show you doing just that. And now I find that you planted your waiter at BistroDimanche in order to implicate the restaurant in the thefts from AFS. It seems you were the one who stole the food, not Dimanche."

Stuart said nothing, and looked away.

Hamish continued. "I found some more of Seamus Dooley's papers. One of them is a letter that requires Seamus to pay you a kickback in cash. You and he had found a way to bilk the Canadian and British forces by inflating the cost of food supplies, hadn't you? You must have met each other because you were doing the same work of provisioning. You realized that since you worked for two different outfits you could use the same invoice twice, perhaps with a little cutting and pasting. Isn't that right?"

Desmond got up and paced the room, clearly agitated. "This is ancient history, Hamish. Why are you raking up things from the past?"

"Because the past doesn't go away, does it, Des? It catches up with you eventually. You thought that you could forget about Seamus Dooley, but then he resurfaced, thanks to your little feud with Serge Dimanche. When I located him, you got very worried. If Dooley was arrested for skipping out from Dimanche's trial, he would reveal that you were the one who put him up to testify against Dimanche in the first place. He kept a record of the sums of money you paid him to do so. And if he revealed the swindle you and he pulled in Germany, you could say goodbye to your British army pension. You could hardly afford to lose it, could you, given the downturn in the restaurant business? Or did he start blackmailing you, and you used me to find out where he was?"

"This is just wild speculation on your part." He glared at Hamish. "I admit that I haven't always played by the rules, but much of what you say is just rubbish!"

"I haven't finished. You decided that you couldn't take the risk of Dooley continuing to ask you for money or being located by the authorities, since he had a lot of incriminating information about you. It would be much better if he just disappeared for good. So you and your associate Joe Arbullo decided to push his truck into the water, with him unconscious in the driver's seat. It must have seemed to you like the perfect crime. Too bad you didn't realize that his tire prints at the side of the road would cast doubt on the story of an accident. Dooley would hardly be likely to miss a turn if he had stopped a few metres from it, would he?"

"I have no idea what you're talking about. I wasn't there."

"Oh, yes you were, Des! The tire prints of a car behind those of Dooley's truck were the tipoff. The treads were from Continental tires, like those on your Audi."

"Nonsense! There must be hundreds of German cars on the road with similar tires. You can't pin Dooley's murder on me–if he was murdered. Why don't you accuse Dimanche? He had a lot to lose from Dooley's testimony. After all, he must have paid him not to testify, which explains why Dooley disappeared. If he was going to reappear, he would be a threat to Dimanche!"

"Your car was photographed by several cameras between here and Rothesay, where Dooley lived, the day before he was found dead. That's surely more than just a coincidence! And I'm sure that the bartender at the Gastropub where he worked will identify you as the man who came asking for Dooley. Face it, Des: you're not going to get away with this!"

Desmond's face turned red in anger. He snarled. "On the contrary! You're the one who isn't going to get away from here alive–and then there won't be anyone left to accuse me of anything." Desmond picked up a brass candlestick, which served as a decoration on the mantle above the fireplace. He advanced toward Hamish and raised the candlestick above his head.

Hamish retreated behind the couch. As he did so, he reached into his pocket. A high-pitched siren blasted intense sound waves, stopping Desmond in his tracks. At the same time, the front door burst open and Sam O'Leary rushed in and wrenched the candlestick from his hand. Desmond fell back, then regained his balance and sprinted toward the front door. Momentarily winded, O'Leary was unable to react in time. The other man lunged outside, only to be tackled by a second policeman who had been waiting near the patrol car. After a brief struggle, the restaurant owner was on the ground, his hands cuffed behind his back.

Hamish sighed with relief. "Thanks, Sam. That was the nick of time. I've got our conversation recorded on my cell phone. It should be enough to convict him, at least of attempted manslaughter."

After reading Desmond his rights, O'Leary and his constable pushed Hamish's assailant into the police cruiser. They then drove him to the main Halifax police station.

38

Back at The Oaks, Hamish reassured Sean and Marjoree that he was OK. "It was touch and go there for a moment though. I was glad that I made sure that Sam would be there to intervene if necessary to stop any violence. In the end, we got what we wanted: an admission of guilt on Desmond's part."

"How were you so sure that it was Desmond who killed Seamus Dooley?" Sean asked. "After all, there was nothing to prove that it was his car rather than Serge's SUV whose tire tracks were found in Rothesay."

"He was very secretive about his past, and denied that he knew Dooley before coming to Halifax, while in fact they had concocted a scheme to defraud the Canadian and British militaries in Germany decades before. Moreover, Dooley sponsored him when he moved to Canada. It seemed likely that he was involved in the latter's disappearance in some way. And Marjoree provided a vital clue when she found that piece of paper in the book that listed 'payments from D'. We assumed that D stood for Dimanche, but when we called the phone number on the piece of paper and found that it connected us to *Bord de l'eau,* it seemed more likely that D stood for Desmond. I came to think that those were bribes from Desmond to get Dooley to testify against the owner of BistroDimanche."

"You took a risk in confronting him. Why not just present the evidence to the police?" Sean wondered.

"I talked it over with Sam O'Leary. We agreed that there wasn't enough to convict him. On the face of it, the video cameras' evidence was damning for Desmond. They put him in the general area of Rothesay at about the time the murder took place. But, if he went to trial, his lawyer would have an easy time arguing that this was purely circumstantial. By that time they would have concocted a story that was at least superficially plausible as to why he was on that road–for instance a trip to Saint John to locate a supplier of some delicacy to serve at his restaurant. However, I thought that if I told him that we had that evidence from the security cameras, he would panic, and he did. His actions proved that he was guilty–though he never actually confessed to the crime. Now the police will need to see if they can find DNA evidence in Desmond's car linking him and Joe Arbullo to Dooley's abduction."

Marjoree patted him on the back. "In any case, we're glad you're safe and sound! So Serge Dimanche was not the bad guy you thought he was. I'm relieved, for Janine's sake. And, you know, I always found him to be fundamentally kind, despite his gruffness and demanding ways. He may have worked for an evil regime in East Germany, but that doesn't mean that he was evil himself."

"He's not off the hook. He's going to have to face the consequences for having suborned a witness. I expect that he will be charged and will have to stand trial. Fortunately, that won't be my responsibility, however."

39

Serge

Serge Dimanche was relaxing on the patio behind his house, admiring the sunset, which was tingeing the western sky in red while casting long shadows behind the red pines on the islands scattered in Mahone Bay. He was still smarting from having been revealed to be Sergei Demanchuk, but happy that at least the detective–Hamish something-or-other–now saw Desmond Stuart for what he was–a wicked, murderous old fool. *He had it in for me when we were rivals for Janine in Germany, and his rancour hasn't abated any since then. Can't he understand that grudges destroy the person who holds them!*

Serge realized now that his run-ins with the law had likely been Desmond Stuart's doing. Seamus Dooley had been bribed by Desmond to testify that he was serving contraband liquor. In the end, Dooley had not been willing to perjure himself, and had run away, thanks to his financial assistance. When Stuart heard from Hamish that Dooley had been found in New Brunswick, the fool had wanted to pay him back for his treachery, as well as to make sure that the truth wouldn't come out. The murder was his downfall.

Serge was now convinced that the waiter who had stolen the steaks from the AFS truck was a setup. He had come to BistroDimanche looking for a job, and Serge had hired him, not suspecting that Desmond wanted to plant him in Serge's organisation in order to frame him for some crime or other. Jimmy had collaborated with another former Stuart employee, Joe Arbullo, to locate the steaks they wanted to steal using an AFS scanner. They knew that the free drink that BistroDimanche offered the driver was the perfect opportunity to get at the truck, and make it look like it was planned by Serge himself.

He didn't regret having moved to Canada and opened the BistroDimanche restaurants. He had been lucky to escape from the GDR and to start fresh with a new name and identity. The last 30 years had been good ones, thanks to Janine's love. They were truly meant for each other. She saw the good in him, and had convinced him that he wasn't all bad. Her kindness and sense of humour had saved him from himself.

Serge noticed that a small wooden sailboat had anchored behind the island nearest to his dock. It was partially hidden by fir trees, and he couldn't see anyone aboard. Local sailors often used the islands for shelter from the prevailing winds, either for a lunch stop or as an overnight anchorage. It might even be someone he knew from the Chester Yacht Club. He reached behind for the binoculars which he kept in a waterproof case on the patio table. He fumbled with the clasp. Before he could take them out, he saw a flash out of the corner of his eye, and felt a sharp pain in his chest. Then he lost consciousness.

Janine heard the shot and rushed out. Blood was spurting out of Serge's chest. Her first impulse was to go to his aid, but she saw right away that it was no use to try to stanch the wound. Instead, she slid on the ground toward him, and grasped his hand. Another bullet ricocheted off the iron table above her. In a panic, she got into a crouch and scrambled for cover in the house. As soon as she was sheltered by the exterior wall, she pulled out her cell phone and called for help. Nine-one-one answered immediately. "My husband's been shot! There's a sniper on a boat near our house. Send the police and an ambulance immediately!"

There were no more shots, so Janine cautiously peered out a window at the water, while staying behind the wall as much as possible. The shooter on the sailboat had turned his back to the house, and was trying to cast off the line tying the boat to a tree. Janine thought, *I can't let him get away without taking a photo of him!* She fumbled for her phone.

Looking at the phone's display to centre the shot while aiming it out the window, she zoomed in on the man in the boat. He had grey hair, and was wearing an old leather jacket and faded jeans. Suddenly she saw another boat appear behind it on the screen, a rigid inflatable boat, or RIB, with the red and white colours of the Canadian Coast Guard. She snapped a photo. Two crewmembers were holding automatic rifles as they bore down on the shooter. After a futile last attempt to get his boat underway, the man on the sailboat put up his hands in a gesture of surrender. Janine collapsed on her living room floor, her fear dissolving as the adrenaline abated, replaced by over-whelming grief at her husband's death.

*****

The ambulance took Serge away, not bothering to put on its flashers because they were not necessary. He had been declared dead at the site by the medical examiner. The cause of death was clear. The Coast Guard had returned to their base, but the RCMP were still at the house. Joe Washington was talking to a detective who was pointing to the place where the gunman had tied up, his boat still visible there. Another officer was extracting a spent bullet from the siding of the house. The shooter, apprehended and handcuffed by the Coast Guard officers, had been turned over to the RCMP when they arrived. He had been taken away in one of the patrol cars.

A policewoman was sitting with Janine in the living room of the house so that she would not be on her own. Janine's face was bathed in tears. "I have no idea who that man was, nor why he would kill my husband." She sobbed. The policewoman stopped talking, letting Janine vent her grief. After a few minutes, she said quietly: "You're lucky that the Coast Guard's Inshore Rescue Boat station for Mahone Bay is nearby, in Chester. They got the nine-one-one call, and rushed over. Otherwise the man might have gotten away. He told us he was paying your husband back for what the Stasi had done to his family in East Germany."

40

The arrested man and presumed assassin of Serge Dimanche had been identified as Gottried Wagner, a naturalized Canadian who had emigrated from Germany in the mid 1990s. He told the police that he had not known Sergei Demanchuk, alias Serge Dimanche, personally, but the mention of him in Tom Gallo's blog prompted Wagner to take his vengeance on a colleague of the Stasi agents who had ruined his life.

Under questioning, he admitted to coming across Tom Gallo's blog by chance when searching for possible outlets for his fruit in Halifax. He learned what he could about Serge Dimanche, and decided that the easiest place to approach him was from the water. An old Enfield rifle had been in the barn of the farm he had purchased. He made sure it was in working condition and practiced shooting at targets. When he was satisfied with his aim he drove to Chester with a small sailboat that he had recently acquired.

Gottfried explained that he had been able to locate Dimanche's house on Mahone Bay on a map. He sailed his dinghy within sight of the house. By chance, its owner was visible on the terrace, so Gottfried did not need to approach further. He lined up the shot as he had practiced doing on his farm, and hit his target in the chest, killing Dimanche instantly.

*****

"Things are certainly very different for me compared to where they were the last time we met," Janine said, looking over at Marjoree. They were sitting at a table having lunch in the Ashcroft Yacht Club's dining room. "Since then, Desmond has been arrested and Serge killed, and now I'm left all alone. We never had any children, and I've lost touch with my relatives in France." She brushed away a tear.

"I'm so sorry for you it had to turn out this way, Janine. I keep thinking that Hamish is partly to blame. If only he hadn't taken that job that Desmond asked him to do! Of course he didn't realize at the time that it was a sort of grudge match between them. But if he hadn't located Seamus Dooley, none of this would have happened."

"Yes, Desmond got him into something that was best kept buried. But how was Hamish to know? He thought Des was his friend, not someone who would manipulate him."

"What will you do with the BistroDimanche business and the house? Do you plan to stay here?"

"I don't know, I haven't been able to think straight since it happened. I might just go back to France for a few months, to see whether I still feel at home there. I might move back if I do. As for the house and boat, I'll put them up for sale. The restaurant business too, if there's any interest. If not, I'll take what I can get for the furnishings and cooking equipment. I don't think the BistroDimanche brand is worth much now."

*****

Marjoree was talking to Hamish and Sean. "I think that Janine will land on her feet. She was the strong one in that couple. She is starting to think of what to do now. She's right to put this part of her life behind her, and move back to Europe."

"You know, this case has soured me on the detective business," Hamish said. "I remember, Sean, that you were leery about taking Desmond's commission. You were right, and it didn't turn out well. I sincerely doubt that we furthered the cause of justice! It's probably true that Serge did some bad things back in East Germany a long time ago. But in my opinion he didn't deserve to die for them now. He did what he had to do to survive in the GDR, and he repented for those actions, going so far as to provide intel to the country's enemies. He was repelled by the things the Stasi did and hated the regime. As for Desmond, he should have let sleeping dogs lie. The attempt to get revenge against his rival ultimately led to his downfall. I should have let sleeping dogs lie too. If I had, Seamus would still be alive, and Desmond would still be in the restaurant business."

"What's going to happen to him?"

"He and Joe Arbullo are going to be tried for first degree murder of Seamus Dooley, and Desmond himself for my attempted murder. The first one may be harder to prove, but the second one should be a slam dunk for the prosecution. The police are still trying to piece together exactly how Seamus was abducted and drowned in his truck. They're no doubt looking for DNA evidence in Desmond's Audi. As for the attempted murder, I'll be called to testify, as will Sam O'Leary. It will be impossible for Desmond's lawyer to contradict the evidence. The police also have an audio recording I made on my cell phone in which he threatened my life."

Sean furrowed his brow. "Are you seriously thinking of abandoning Cameron and Carroll, Investigators? This case may have gone wrong, but don't forget we did bring to justice a number of bad guys over the years, starting with Jerry Adams and Guy Laframboise at the New Dawn retirement home. We saved Kristy Oliveira from a terrible fate, and cleaned up the drug problem at the high school. Not to mention breaking up that UModel scam that exploited gullible women, and exposing evil deeds related to the African country of Summerland! All of those cases led to good outcomes. Please reconsider quitting the detective business, Hamish. "

"Let's think about it."

"If you wanted to give some of the work to a younger person, I know someone who would make a good detective. Her name is Beth Phillips, and she figured out how the people who robbed the AFS truck knew where to look. She has a good head on her shoulders."

"And, I gather, a cute body below them!" Hamish laughed, while looking disapprovingly at Sean.

41

Epilogue

The case against Desmond Stuart and Joe Arbullo for the murder of Seamus Dooley was, as Hamish had feared, based mainly on circumstantial evidence. Desmond's car was captured on camera close to the site of Seamus's death, and they were identified as the two men who had asked for him at the Gastropub. But there was no evidence that they had entered his house or hijacked his truck, and they had been careful not to put him into the Audi, so there was no DNA evidence there.

The break in the case against Stuart came from a plea bargain with Arbullo. The two of them had been accused of conspiring to defraud AFS by stealing valuable produce from its trucks. The discovery of the scanner by Sean had provided the police evidence that the two of them had been involved in the theft. In exchange for leniency in that case, Arbullo testified that he had indeed accompanied Stuart to Dooley's home, thinking that they were just going to talk to him to make sure that he didn't reveal his past dealings with Desmond to the police. When Dooley came to the door, they forced their way in, and an altercation led to him being knocked unconscious. Desmond ordered Arbullo to drag Dooley out to his truck, Desmond got into it, and told Joe to follow in Desmond's car to a place where they would leave him. Joe claimed to the police that he imagined that this was just a form of intimidation, and that Desmond would not harm Dooley. They drove for some time, eventually reaching a crossroads, where Desmond pulled off the road. Joe parked Desmond's Audi in back of the truck and waited. He witnessed Desmond push Seamus, who was still lying unconscious on the passenger side of the F-150, into the driver's seat. Then he put the truck's shift lever into drive, and pushed Dooley's leg down onto the accelerator. As the truck started down the hill toward the water, Desmond slammed its door and stepped back. The truck bounced down the incline and ploughed into the lake, gradually sinking as the water filled up its cab and cargo hold.

Arbullo claimed that he was shocked by what happened to Dooley, and that he did not have any inkling beforehand that Desmond would send the Ford F-150 down the hill into the water in order to drown his former collaborator. Apparently the jury found his testimony convincing. Desmond was convicted of murder and sentenced to life imprisonment, while Joe himself received a lesser sentence.

Desmond's conviction for attempting to murder Hamish was thus icing on the cake. In any case, Stuart was going to spend the rest of his life behind bars.

Hamish still rued the day he had accepted Desmond's commission to investigate Serge Dimanche, but decided to stay in the detective business with Sean. He vowed to be more careful in accepting cases, and agreed with Sean to let Beth join their firm to learn the ropes as a detective so that over time she could take over some of his work. Marjoree of course was not pleased but reluctantly accepted her as a co-worker, while herself remaining at Cameron and Carroll as office manager. Time would tell whether this arrangement would last or not.

Janine moved back to France and opened a BistroDimanche restaurant in suburban St. Cloud to honour the memory of her husband. Surprisingly, it did rather well, thanks to her hiring the former chef at *Bord de l'eau*, the rugby player Roland Lepage. The restaurant was an upscale version, with a varying and innovative menu, of the Halifax BistroDimanche. It became a popular destination for Parisians visiting the Parc de St. Cloud on Sundays, and after a few years it even earned a Michelin star. The Nova Scotia chain of restaurants was abandoned, the bad publicity and the after-effects of covid having made it unprofitable. Desmond Stuart's restaurant *Bord de l'eau* went into receivership and was turned into an Irish pub.

The trial of Gottfried Wagner was delayed in order to perform a detailed psychological examination of Serge Dimanche's assassin. Reviving his memories of persecution by the Stasi in the GDR had unhinged him, and he seemed to have lost his awareness of where he now lived. He did not recall coming to Canada, nor of hunting down and killing Serge Dimanche. He spoke incessantly about wanting to go to the Thomaskirche to listen to music. Eventually, the Public Prosecution Service judged that he was not fit to stand trial, and he was instead lodged in a psychiatric hospital. At the suggestion of his doctor, he was given an MP3 player and recordings of the works of J.S. Bach, and he spent his days listening with childlike joy to the music of the master.

About the Author

I am a retired economist living in Niagara-on-the-Lake, Ontario, and have published extensively on various aspects of international economics and macroeconomic policy, including an analysis of the economic effects of German reunification.

My hobbies include running, gardening, kayaking, and sailing. My sailboat, *Fugue*, is berthed at the Niagara-on-the-Lake Sailing Club.

More information about my detective series, *The ABC Files*, can be found on my website, **paulmassonwebsite.com**. I would welcome your feedback: you can email me using the "Contact Us" form there. To receive advance notice of new novels and a prequel of the ABC Files click the Newsletter sign up page.

My detective novels can be found on Amazon and on Goodreads. If you enjoyed this book, please consider submitting a review.

www.ingramcontent.com/pod-product-compliance
Lightning Source LLC
Chambersburg PA
CBHW021710190726
48289CB00008B/2461